KILL SWITCH

The Third Anna Harris Novel

A V IAIN

Chapter One

THE GENTLE *HUM* of computer cooling fans sounds all around me.

Monitors—left on overnight—cast a slick, bluish glow over the office.

Flickering, twisting shadows.

The air isn't exactly warm, but it's warm enough to bring the sweat oozing out of my pores. To allow the fresh, peachy scent of my deodorant to work its magic. I comb my fingers through my hair; pulled-back into a smart, sensible ponytail. Shove a few loose strands back into place, beneath the tie.

Next, I reach up and pull back the elasticated neck of my black, skin-tight Lycra top with my index finger. Get in a couple of deep breaths.

Then I continue.

I keep myself low, crouched down and away from the windows of the building. Prowling about in the darkness like a cat. Although it's the early hours of a London morning, and the sun won't be up any time soon, I can't be too careful. There might be someone in one of the buildings across the street working at this time. These *City* people have notoriously bizarre timetables: doing business with Hong Kong, or Sydney; God knows where else.

When I get to the end of the current office space—filled with flimsy-walled cubicles, each of them with a dozen or so workstations nestled inside—I glance back over my shoulder, sure that I'm being followed.

But, most likely, it's just paranoia.

And paranoia—on occasion—can get you killed.

I reach down to my waist, to my belt there, and I feel for the handgun I have holstered.

.45 calibre.

Silencer already fitted.

Given to me by my employer, earlier today.

I named it, imaginatively, *Punisher*.

Punisher is all ready for *killing*.

My employer, Brian Mathewson: publicist and owner, director, gravy-maker—and any other role you might care to name—of Mathewson Media; gave me the information on this hit only a few hours ago. In a brown, A4-sized envelope. I recall looking over the office plan, memorising it, looking to the red ring, scrawled out in felt pen, the place where the target will be waiting.

The person I've been sent to kill.

As I feel the white-washed wall behind me, beneath the touch of my leather gloves, I can still taste the tomato sauce off the pasta I wolfed down about an hour ago. I've learned, being a cold-blooded assassin, that skipping meals is a false economy. It leads to shaking. To getting sloppy.

In short, nothing good.

The air here smells strongly of paper and glue, and I can't help but cast my mind back to my school days, to those odours which I associate with overheated classrooms in summer. Now, though, they're reset in this context.

In this *killing* context.

My plimsolls make hardly a sound as I tread over the thread-bare office carpet in the hallway, the pinewood door in my sight. I can see that this company keeps a tight clutch on its expenses. A *sensibly* run business.

And one which—come tomorrow—shall find one of its employees dead.

As I approach the door, I unbutton the holster for my handgun.

Slip my gun out.

Feel its bulky weight.

Balance it on instinct.

I reach out for the doorknob, telling myself to make this quick, to simply act on instinct, as any predator would do. There're no doubts any more. Not at this stage.

My head is *all* sorted out.

. . . Or that's the theory.

I can almost hear each individual muscle in my hand twitching as I turn the doorknob. The weight of my gun becomes almost impossibly heavy. I hold it up in my grip, point it to the door, ready to fire.

And that's when I feel cold, hard steel up against my neck.

The voice which tells me to, *Freeze, or else!*

Chapter Two

I HOLD UP MY HANDS.

Surrender my gun.

Not much else I can do.

As I stand there, very much exposed, I note my adversary's posture, physical makeup. I can't help noticing that they're short —*compact*. When I catch sight of the flesh beyond the squeezed-on leather gloves, I see that it's a skinny wrist.

Snow-white skin.

Well-*moisturised* skin.

Another woman?

As that thought passes across my mind space, I hear the voice.

"Turn around, Anna."

I do as I'm told and, since I'm not asked to look away, I don't.

I look up, over the gun being pointed at me.

Stare right back into the face.

Into *her* face.

Blond hair.

Held tightly in a bun.

Muscular frame.

Quite small . . . at the very least a few centimetres off my height.

Her eyes are a sapphire-blue, and a strong scent of strawberries blasts through the air.

In her mid-to-late twenties, maybe younger.

Younger than me at least.

She feeds me a smile, wiggling her nose as she does so.

For several seconds, a kind of déjà vu passes through me.

Then realisation hits.

I *know* this woman . . . this *girl* . . .

"Amy?" I just about manage to get out.

"Been a while, hasn't it, Anna?"

"But," I add, my eyes searching her face, the gun that she holds up to my chest, "You're *police*."

That's an understatement, Amy—or Amy *Douglas* as I know her from before—is the daughter of Charlie Branwick, or, as he's professionally known: Chief Constable Branwick.

The last time I saw Amy she was dressed in a uniform—a *police* uniform—albeit disappearing in my rear-view mirror, treading her way up a garden path of a house to go kill the owner who, consequently, had recently murdered his wife.

A client of Brian's, he had been all set to get away with it.

To say that Amy has a strong moral compass is putting it lightly.

Amy gives a shrug, tilts her head to one side and squints as if she's having trouble focussing on me. "Not anymore."

I stare down at the gun in her hand, notice that it's the same as my own: another forty-five. My eyes, on instinct, drift down to her belt too. I see an ugly, grey, lumpy metal object strapped on there.

A grenade?

I look back up, into her eyes. "Who sent you here—to kill me?"

Amy holds my gaze over the top of the gun. She squints harder now, and I recall something about her being long-sighted, one of those strange, unruly nuggets of information that jumps up and strikes me every so often.

She lowers the gun.

Smiles wider.

"I'm not here to kill you, Anna," she says.

My heart raps at the base of my tongue. "So why the whole sneaking-around act?"

Amy stares back at me, the gun down at her side now. "It wasn't my idea."

"Then whose was it?" I say, and then, not giving her the chance to respond to that question, add, "*Brian's.*"

Amy reaches out her hand, the one which she holds my gun in.

She offers my gun to me.

I take it gladly. I look it over, checking that everything's in place. It is. Then I return it to the holster on the back of my belt. "So, I'm guessing there's no target at all?"

Amy shakes her head. She breathes in deeply, and then sighs out, turning her back to me, as if something about this night-time office has caught her attention. As if there's something *infinitely* more interesting happening here than her conversation with me.

I have to admit, I'm not much enjoying this *impromptu* reunion.

"How long have you been working with him—with Brian?"

" 'With Brian?' "

"How long have you been working this job?" I say, putting it as bluntly as I dare in this office, no doubt packed with all sorts of concealed surveillance devices.

Amy stifles a yawn with the back of her free hand, the one which *doesn't* grip her gun. "Oh, I'd say I've been doing jobs for Brian—among *others*—for a year or so, give or take."

" 'Others?' " I say, my turn to be the parrot.

"That's the thing with freelance," she says, "it's not good practice to rely on one client alone."

I feel a slight bite to that comment . . . all right, more than just a *slight* bite.

Because I only have one client—Brian wouldn't allow me to have any more.

"You see," Amy continues, "that's the good thing about being the Chief Constable's daughter, it buys you all sorts of privileges not available to the working assassin."

"I don't . . ." I get out, unable to really put into words my confusion.

Amy turns back to me, away from the—apparently *fascinating*—darkness she was staring into. "We both agreed—my *daddy* and me"—I can't help noticing the stress she puts on 'daddy'—"that I might not be cut out for the police." Amy's eyes widen, her lips part momentarily. "That I might not have the patience for it—that I might be just a touch *volatile*."

I say nothing, very aware that she still squeezes her gun down by her side, in her grip, and that it'd take only a swift flick for her to bring it back onto me.

If she has the protection that she's intimating—or even if she *feels* that she has the protection—I don't want to do anything to get her to test out that 'volatile' nature of hers.

"So, me and *Daddy*"—there's that stress again—"we decided that I might be able to make my way through *other* means . . . you see," she continues, taking a couple of steps towards me, "I've always had this sense, this *desire* to pull a trigger.

"To *snuff* someone's life out."

I hold off for as long as I'm able without replying.

Then I can't resist.

"Yeah," I say, "it's called a Kill Switch."

Chapter Three

TEN MINUTES LATER, and the two of us stand within the office—the one which'd been marked as being the target for tonight.

Amy reaches down for her belt. For one terrible second, I'm certain that she's going to rip that grenade free, toss it and kill the both of us. But, instead, she produces this fancy illumination device—I think it'd be damning it with faint praise to call it a 'torch'—and places it down on the table.

A flood of bluish-white, even light fills the office.

The office is a standard, windowless, charmless affair. A computer set on a dainty desk. The legs of the desk look like they'd *snap* if only the user thought to rest their elbows to type.

"Just wondering," I say, "but why'd you bring a grenade along?"

"Oh, that?" Amy says, her gaze slipping down to her belt. She snaps her head back up, her lips erupting in a smile. "That's just smoke—useful on occasion."

"What're you?" I say. "Some sort of ninja?"

Amy just gives me a shrug and a smile as she busies herself with the computer, tapping away, her leather gloves snug on her hands. Apparently she knows what she's doing. As she types, I notice a few frown lines in her forehead and wonder how they might've got there.

Surely not stress?

Surely this assassin's gig isn't like a dreaded *real* job?

I say nothing as she bashes the keyboard, the keys filling the room with that plastic *clickety-click*. When I breathe in now, I can only taste mint. I shovelled a couple of strips of gum in through my lips realising that I'm going to be in company . . . company which I'm going to be around for longer than the squeezing of a trigger.

I feel the steady weight of my handgun on my belt and reach around, rest my hands at my lower back. These past few weeks I've been feeling all tense down there, and I've been wondering why.

At first I thought it might be my back telling me to get a new mattress—one which hasn't been reduced to pulp—but when I did acquire a new mattress, not an interesting or *enjoyable* task by any means, swapped it out for one about as hard as an ironing board, I noticed no difference whatsoever.

Maybe I should get the number of a good chiropractor.

Who knows, they might be male and attractive . . .

"Anna?" Amy says.

I glance over to her, away from a cheaply framed charcoal drawing I was pretending to be entranced by. That fancy illumination device of Amy's makes it easy to pick out all the contours of the charcoal, each and every one of the artist's hand strokes. The picture depicts a placid-looking bay which brings to mind

San Floriano, the Spanish beach where I spent a—not entirely relaxing—couple of weeks, a year or so ago.

I tread over to Amy, stand at her shoulder and look over the computer screen.

Filled with line-upon-line of code:

White text on black background.

It means nothing to me.

I look to Amy. "Not convinced I'll be much help with this."

Amy rolls her eyes. "Not that," she says, and then gestures downwards, to the desk.

To something which lies on the desk.

When I get down to look, squinting a little against the fierce, blue-white light from the illumination device, I see that it's a little book. A pocket-sized book:

Leather-bound.

A slight burgundy shade.

Gold-edged pages.

It looks a little like one of those pocket diaries people would use to keep track of dates and times last century . . . before the bittersweet popular take-up of the computer—and the internet.

I look to Amy again.

"Take it," she says, her attention back on the computer screen.

Her fingers go *clickety-click* again over the keyboard.

"Where'd you find it?" I say.

"In one of the drawers," Amy replies casually, without breaking pace with her rapid-fire typing. "It might be helpful," she adds, with a smile tweaking her lips as she stabs the Enter key, then crouches down and slips a USB drive out of a slot in the computer.

I shrug and thrust the book into my pocket.

"Come on," Amy says, taking me by the hand in a somewhat school girl-like manner, "we need to go."

As we make our way out of the office complex, down the stairs which run around the back of the building, I find myself in an unlikely—*uncommonly*—talkative mood.

Grasping the banister with my leather-gloved hands, not wanting to take any risk of taking a tumble, I say, "Where'd you manage to pick up those computer skills?"

Amy shrugs as if it's nothing important.

As if she *hasn't* just blown my mind right open with the speed of her typing alone.

"Cyber Crimes Unit," she replies, reaching the bottom step.

I partially open my mouth to indicate comprehension. But since she doesn't look back, and I don't *really* feel as if she's answered my question—not to my dim-witted brain—it seems like a somewhat wasted gesture.

Before I know it, we're flying out through the exterior door, back into the darkness:

The car park which runs around the back of the building.

Surrounded by the looming, giant shadows of oak trees.

Chapter Four

I CAN HEAR MY PHONE buzzing its merry way across the surface of my bedside table and, although I'm still half asleep, and at least half convinced that I have the telekinetic powers I was just dreaming about, I'm confused at why it won't hang up the call.

Another couple of seconds later and I snap awake.

Sit up straight in bed.

Press my shoulders up against the headboard, and feel the sturdy support against my back.

Before I've even consciously given the matter any thought, my hand launches itself to my forehead. My touch is chilly, but soothing. It feeds me a much-needed dose of reality.

My son Ben's football match.

My mouth tastes stale. My tongue is like a sodden piece of sponge. I reach out for my phone. See that there're three missed calls. All from my ex-husband: Arnold. Just as I stare at the screen with something like horror, the phone begins to rumble again. Acting on instinct more than anything else, I accept the call.

Press the handset to my ear.

"Arnold?" I say.

"Brian," Brian Mathewson, my employer, replies.

I blink several times. Bring my disordered bedroom in focus:

Clothes of all kinds strewn across the floor; beige-white walls, scuffmarks all over; and the way I never seem to get around to shutting the door to my wardrobe, constantly exposing those hordes and hordes of shoes threatening to tumble out.

" 'Brian?' " I reply, giving myself another few blinks to get fully shot of my daze.

As if he might have my bedroom wired for video, I prise myself out from beneath my duvet, leaving it in a ragged pile on the floor, and I stride up to the window. A yank of a cord later and the slatted blinds fly upwards with a *shoock* sound.

I glance out through the window, see that the sky is grizzly and grey, that a fine drizzle is falling. A perfect day to stay inside —to stay *in bed* . . . whoever came up with the concept that makes it okay to play football in the rain needs his head examined . . . and it most likely *was* a *he* . . .

"Did you have a good time last night?" Brian says.

His tone is somewhat jovial.

Far happier than he should be.

Or should that be *pleased with himself* . . .

"Uh huh," I say, staring out into the rain, already thinking about having to throw an anorak about my shoulders; needing to pop open an umbrella and just get *out* there.

I feel something warm, and furry, and *purring*, wrap itself about my legs.

I glance down and see Lizzie, my tortoiseshell cat.

Knowing it's the only way to see off this display—short of ripping open a pouch of cat food—I bend down and gather her up in my arms, squeezing my mobile between my ear and my shoulder so that I can still make out whatever Brian's got to say for himself.

Lizzie feels a little *lumpier* than usual, or maybe it's just my imagination.

I turn my attention back to Brian.

"It was, uh," I say, pausing to think for a second, *"funny."*

On the other end of the line, I hear Brian clap his hands together. He sends a chuckle down the line—a chuckle which makes my stomach quiver just a little. There's something about Brian and that merry laugh of his that I've never been all that comfortable around.

"I thought you should get to know one another," Brian says, "since you'll be working together for the foreseeable future— thought that it might be fun for you to meet up in that shutdown office."

Even as I think the words, I know that I should know better— that an ex-Army girl like me should know the consequences of insubordination . . . but I can't help myself. "Don't you think that it was a little risky?" I say. "I mean, how can you be sure that nobody was listening in to what we were saying?"

"Oh, come off it, old girl," Brian replies, "you will have been quite all right—in actual fact that building is one of mine."

I feel a few of the knots in my muscles unwind themselves.

I'm glad to hear that.

And, in truth, I would've been probably just as glad to have heard that *before* setting foot in that office . . . last night, when I got home, when I slipped myself into bed, I did an awful lot of tossing and turning thinking about the things that I might've said —*shouldn't have said*—to Amy in some anonymous office.

I look away from the dismal scene out the window, perhaps half believing that if I cease to think about the weather it'll clear itself up on its own. I stare long and hard at the walls of my bedroom and think about repainting them . . . or perhaps I could call a painter in.

"Anyway," Brian goes on, "I didn't want to trample on your Saturday plans, nothing like that, but I would quite like for you to pop into my office sometime this afternoon—how about four o'clock?"

"Sounds fine," I say, slotting that appointment away in my brain. I hold myself off for a couple of seconds before asking, "Will *she* be there too?"

"Who?" Brian says, playing the innocent.

"*Amy.*"

Brian chuckles again. "Is that just a hint of jealousy I can hear?" He takes a swig of something—whisky?—and then says, "Yes, I thought that we should have a formal briefing together later on . . . make sure we're all on the same page, sound good?"

"Fine," I say, and then hang up.

Lizzie wriggles in my arms and I let her loose. She shoots on out through my bedroom door and downstairs.

I've only just laid my phone down on my bedside table when it begins to buzz all over again. As I reach down to pick it up, down at my feet, among all my scrunched-up clothing—the clothes I wore the night before—I spot the burgundy diary.

Still staring at the diary, I snatch up my phone.

Press it to my ear once again.

Chapter Five

ALTHOUGH I HATE to do it—to be *that* employee—I
call up the Mathewson Media carpool and get a car sent
by to pick me up.

Arnold wasn't angry on the phone—he's *never* angry—but he
was the closest he ever gets to it. That's to say that he was *anxious*
to know where I was.

Ben's football match starts within the hour.

In theory, the kids are meant to get to the football pitch an
hour before the start of the match, for warmups, or whatever . . .
Oops.

Five minutes later, and a brand-new, silver estate with tinted
windows pulls up at the curb outside my ex-Council house.

I hurl myself into the back seat, not even having had time to
throw my anorak about my shoulders. I toss my bundled-up
waterproof off onto the other side of the seat, first doing a
cursory check to see if there's anyone else sitting there . . . I have
to admit that anytime I happen to be stepping into a car with

tinted windows it's always with a somewhat half expectation that there'll already be someone sat inside—*waiting* for me.

The air smells lightly of car freshener and leather, from the seats.

My mouth feels a little burned from the tea I wolfed down on my way out the door. I catch a slight taste of blood mixed with tea towards the back of my throat.

The driver says absolutely nothing to me beyond asking for the address and giving me a curt nod. I slip a little on the leather seat from the force of acceleration, and somehow manage to hook my seatbelt around me before we take the corner up ahead.

As we shuttle along the road, I pad my pockets, feel the diary there, and I slip it out.

Even though I'm late enough not to have had time to take a shower, I somehow *did* have the presence of mind to slip the diary, which Amy pilfered the night before, into the pocket of my jeans. As I open the cover, I notice a tea stain down the front of my light-blue, V-necked shirt, and I think, *Classy, Anna.* At least I've brought my anorak along to cover the stain. From my experience of other children's parents—*especially mothers*—one's appearance is of utmost importance . . . even on a chilly Saturday morning in October.

I read the first page of the diary, scrawled handwriting, red ink, all loopy and joined up in an elegant manner which, I'm ashamed to say, I still struggle with.

Even at thirty-six.

I squint at the page for several minutes, taking a long time in attempting to decipher the message—a word at a time—and mostly failing.

As we round yet another corner, I hear the driver's voice,

glance up and see his eyes peering back at me in the rear-view mirror. "Forgot your glasses?"

"What?" I say.

The driver gives me a smirk and then taps the sunglasses he's wearing. "Might want to go and get them tested—you're wrinkling the whole of your face trying to read that."

I put on my best polite smile and say, "That's something to think about—thank you."

The driver turns his attention back to his assigned task:

Driving.

When I hear the driver's voice again, I feel myself—*quietly*—beginning to boil with anger . . . I can't quite deal with people at this time in the morning, especially when I've been robbed of a decent proportion of my beauty sleep.

But, this time, it's only to inform me that we've arrived at Arnold's house.

What *used to be* my house.

I glance out the window to see that my son Ben's already sitting on the doorstep, chin resting on his kneecaps, boot bag clenched between his trainers. I suppose the world's a smaller, much simpler place when you're a thirteen-year-old boy—when most of your waking thoughts are occupied with football.

I remember that the car windows are tinted, I tap the button to wind the window down and it does its job with a flat, nasal *whine.*

A little drizzle sneaks into the car as I peer out across the garden. It's beginning to go a little feral in the winter rains, I note, a touch smugly. Still, though, when I breathe in, I can smell the thick scent of rose petals in the air. And those earthy tones which fill me with such a pleasant sense of wellbeing that they make me consider—*come spring*—whether I should plant my own garden.

Or pay someone to do so.

When Ben spots me, he glances back over his shoulder.

I realise that the front door is open a crack.

He calls back into the house.

Every muscle in my body seizes up tight—if there's *anything* I would rather avoid this morning, it's a face-off with Arnold and his partner, *Kate*.

Silently, I will Ben to his feet, and away from the door, and he does get a few steps away before the door opens up fully, to reveal Kate standing there:

Her black hair . . . a little longer than last time I saw it.

Those sparkling blue eyes.

That *delicate* posture of hers.

I feel myself drawing even tenser still when Kate produces a flask and then, scrubbing up Ben's hair, hands it to him.

Ben tilts his head to one side, attempting to avoid the mussing, but there's little he can do to prevent it. As Ben approaches the car at a light jog, the flask in hand, I open the door for him. And I find myself, for a few paralysing moments, forced into giving Kate a sort of half wave as she stands there on the doorstep.

Thankfully, the driver seems to grasp the subtleties of the situation.

He stamps the accelerator and speeds off, away from the house.

———

I'd like to say that the weather improves when we get to the football pitch but, actually, pretty much the opposite is true. The rain falls a little heavier, the air grows a little colder, and I find myself longing to return to the car—parked up only fifty or so metres away—to bundle myself up in the back seat, and wait for the final whistle.

But there is such a thing as *moral* support at stake.

Even if that moral support involves me watching Ben— wearing a high-vis, lime-green bib over his red-and-black football shirt—do galloping sidesteps along the opposite touchline with the other substitutes for his team.

Despite my limited knowledge of football, even *I* know that the fact that Ben's team have allowed the opposition to put the ball in their goal three—*or is four?*—times isn't a good thing.

I look to the manager of Ben's team, watch him give his bald, drizzle-drenched head a couple of scratches as he—*apparently*— masterminds a comeback.

"Nice day for it."

The voice is chirpy—*too chirpy*—and sounds almost as if it's *convinced* of the truth of what, surely, must be an *ironic* comment.

I turn to look.

Find myself temporarily dumbstruck.

Standing there beside me, is a large man—broad-shouldered, with thick, black hair hanging down the back of his neck; *soaked*, of course. He wears a brown, oilskin overcoat and has his hands shoved into the pockets. Every second I spend staring at him, it seems as if he's growing another centimetre.

Feeling my heart flutter up to my throat, a slight blush entering my cheeks, I turn my attention back to the football match playing out before us.

Ben *still* isn't playing.

"What are you?" I reply. "A *duck?*"

The man gives a chesty laugh to my lame joke.

I come to the conclusion that he's extremely patient with the humour-impaired.

Or hitting on me.

"Which one's your boy?" he says.

I shrug my shoulders, not because I don't care, but because, if I don't, my shuddering might crush me from the outside in. "The one over there, in the construction-site gear."

Again, the man laughs.

Yes, *extremely* patient . . . or *extremely* desperate.

"Mine's the one over there," the man says, pointing to the football pitch and then—*helpfully*—adding, "Number nine."

I make out the raven-haired boy with the white number nine on his shorts. In many ways, but most of all his *height*, he's a spitting image of his father. The boy is red-cheeked and he stands with his hands impatiently on his hips.

I suppose he's unhappy with the direction this match is taking.

"He looks . . ." I search for a suitable observation ". . . *cold*."

"Your lad," the man goes on, "Ben, isn't it?"

"Uh huh."

"He's pretty good—he should be playing—he's started every match this season."

I think back to the lashings of scowls, not to mention the sustained silence, I got off Ben as we drove here, to the football pitch. He didn't even reply to me when I wished him good luck, he just slipped on off the back seat and jogged over to join his teammates.

The man sighs. "Suppose he got here a little too late—got *disciplined*."

"Yes," I say, hoping this conversation winds up soon, "I suspect that's it."

There's a long, *yawning* silence between the two of us, and I hope the fact that I don't pick up the slack in the conversation communicates to this man—*somehow*—that, really, I'm not interested in anything he has to say.

However, it seems to have the opposite effect.

"Pardon me for saying, but I've never seen you about here before, bringing Ben along to the football. He usually comes along with his dad, and his mum" . . . here I shift a glaring glance in the man's direction, and he seems to see the error of his ways . . . "I mean, *you're* his mum, I suppose?"

I see that his cheeks have coloured a little now.

And not from the cold.

Hopefully I can force him into a full retreat.

"Yes, you could suppose that," I reply.

He nods to me, meets my eye for a moment, and I realise that he has—*quite lovely*—hazel-brown eyes, with flecks of green scattered about his irises. He looks away, back to the pitch. "Modern families, eh?" He holds himself still—*almost stiff*—and then he says, "My wife, she" . . . his throat seems to clog with something, and then he swallows it back . . . "a year ago now, she left us, she *passed away*."

Great, now *I* feel like the bad guy.

Since there's not much I can do, I continue to stand beside the man—who introduces himself as 'Mark, Nathan's father.' When he reaches out to shake my hand, I feel that his skin is calloused, but not unpleasantly so. He has what my dad would've called 'honest hands.' He goes on to tell me that he's a carpenter. That he puts together various wooden handicrafts. When I ask him whether he might be able to put together a chair for my cat, he takes me seriously and promises that he will.

The referee gives a hard toot on his whistle and the boys all gather together into huddles on the pitch—ostensibly to discuss strategy, or whatever titbits they need to chat about before the beginning of the next half.

When I breathe in now, I catch that slightly revolting stench of damp fabric—from my anorak—and though I've warmed to Mark at least a little, I can't help but feel that his oilskin overcoat smells a little of wet dog.

Now that I'm standing on the side lines, beside a man who I'm now on first-name terms with, I wish that I'd taken a quick shower before flying out the door. But, then again, if I'd dawdled even a minute longer, who knows what sort of punishment Ben would've faced from his—apparently *totalitarian*—coach.

I offer Mark a strip of gum which he accepts from me. Soon enough, the smooth, minty waves pass through my mouth, throb through my tongue, and begin to make me feel almost human again.

Having Mark standing nearby certainly has its advantages, seeing as I seem to catch a little of his body warmth . . . or maybe it's because my blood is slowly turning to ice, and I'm beginning to forget what warmth even is anymore.

"Hang on a sec," Mark says, holding his hand up to me.

I watch on as Mark crosses the pitch, strides all the way up to Ben's bald-headed coach. The bald-headed coach doesn't, as I'd anticipated, turn on Mark with a sincerely fed-up expression; rather he fires him a bright smile. They chat about something for the best part of a minute, and then Mark turns around, returns to my side.

Like a faithful stray.

"What was that about?" I say.

Mark shrugs, looking on at the pitch as the boys break from their huddle, and take up their positions for the second half of the match. "Just told him that I thought your boy should get a go now." He turns full on to face me, those hazel eyes of his now having made the steep transition from *merely alluring* to *irresistible*. "Said that he's been punished enough."

I feel my chest squeeze tight, my ribs seeming as if they're trying their best to crush my heart and lungs. But I turn back to the match before Mark catches a clue.

Or that's what I hope.

Chapter Six

THE MATCH FINISHES three-three, and, on the ride back to Arnold's house, Ben leads me through a blow-by-blow account of just what happened, and how he and Mark's son —*Nathan*—'linked up' well.

It seems as if my late arrival has been forgotten when I give him a quick kiss goodbye, and he flurries out of the back seat, and patters along the garden path, back up to the front door. I tell the driver to go before the door opens.

I go back home to change, grab a bite to eat, and the driver pulls up outside my house—as arranged—at about three o'clock. Together, we drive to Mathewson Media, and the driver drops me at the lift in the underground car park.

I take the lift up to the thirteenth floor.

Famous for his secretarial turnover, Brian had a redhead installed earlier this year. She has a penchant for turquoise and silver—today she wears a turquoise blouse, with a frilly front, with all her fingernails painted turquoise to match. She has on some silver bracelets and a pair of silver earrings. When she glances up from her computer screen, she's unsmiling and tells me to take a seat.

As I sit there, on the white leather sofa, I think about the sensible, navy-blue pinstriped trouser suit I picked out to wear for the meeting today. And I wonder how I'm going to stand up in comparison to Amy. I hardly have time to think about that, though, because Amy herself appears—*clicking* and *clacking*—at the end of the hallway.

I see that she's wearing a scarlet cocktail dress, one which—I imagine—hardly covers the lower crest of her buttocks. Her blond hair dangles down, sheening in the afternoon sunlight which beams in through the corridor windows. She's *extremely* well made-up and she grips tightly to the golden chain of a small clutch purse which dangles from her fingertips.

Without a word to me, Amy reaches out and seizes hold of my wrist, pulling me up from my seat with some kind of super-natural strength.

Her thick, strawberry scent is almost overpowering today.

I wonder if the woman's on steroids.

Or maybe she's just making the most of not having to wear a police uniform any longer.

Together, me trailing in her wake, and with Brian's secretary giving the pair of us a deeply worried glance but saying nothing, Amy grabs hold of the golden handles to the doors of Brian's office and gives them a twist.

Without any resistance, and a gargled protest from the secretary—lost in the *creak* of the door's hinges—Amy strides into Brian's office.

I slip the secretary an apologetic expression, and then close the doors quietly, but *firmly* behind me.

Weak, autumnal sunlight beams in through the windows—three quarters of the wall space in Brian's thirteenth floor office. The sunlight sets Brian in its golden rays. Today he's wearing a silky suit, black, and it, too, shimmers in the sun. Brian is on the phone, staring out through the glass, across the cityscape. He has his signature tumbler of whisky clutched down at his side. A little beyond Brian, I can make out Parliament Square. Bristling, leafy trees line the streets, their leaves only now beginning to turn a little yellow about the edges.

Smooth, ivory-white marble pillars prop up the ceiling of the office—seeming to meld nicely into the standard Mathewson Media décor, what makes up the rest of the building, but, at the same time, to clash with just about everything else in the office *here*.

There's a smoky, woody smell coming from somewhere and, when I look to the pinewood drinks cabinet—covered in rings from uncoastered glasses laid down there—I realise that he's burning a joss stick. I wonder at that detail for a moment, not ever having pinned Brian as being the hippy type—or having any sort of patience for anything related to hippiedom.

Then again, I guess you learn new things about people every day.

And, when it comes to Brian, he's a deep, unfathomable ocean.

Although we've just burst into his office without so much as knocking, Brian slips me and Amy a delighted glance, gives a mock salute, and then turns his attention back to the phone call he's having. As I draw my attention away from him, I realise that Amy's staring at me—that she's giving me something approaching a smirk.

I know that she's *extremely* pleased about what she's achieved here.

That she's *shown* me that she can do whatever she wants around Brian.

Her daddy—the Chief Constable—will protect her.

With a few extremely haughty—not to mention *false*—laughs, Brian hangs up the call. He playfully slaps his mobile down on the surface of his drinks cabinet, then pours himself another whisky. As always, Brian's cheeks are a touch rosy. He grins in mine and Amy's direction. "Afternoon, ladies, I can't thank you enough for dropping by."

I glance to Amy, see that—already—she's prowling towards Brian, like a, very much untamed, wildcat.

I have the urge to roll my eyes, but don't.

Her strawberry fragrance is doing battle with Brian's wood-scented joss sticks and is—*seemingly*—winning.

"Uncle Bry," Amy croons, leaning into Brian, her lips brushing a rosy cheek.

Brian colours a little more—the dirty old sod—and when Amy finally steps away from him, he is grinning so widely it's any wonder he doesn't split open his skull. As a sort of afterthought, he turns his gaze over to me. "Anna!" he says, seemingly using every last gasp remaining in his lungs to do so.

I'm not so easily fooled.

Brian looks between me and Amy, then indicates the area of his office he's had recently—to my eye—renovated:

A brand-new, sofa-and-armchair set. All of the items made of a powder-blue velvet fabric.

At least it *feels* like velvet to my untrained touch.

A dainty, glass coffee table sits between us all, a shagpile rug underneath. There's a pile of gossip rags on top of the coffee table; all of them, no doubt, representing a good job *well done* for Brian.

Nothing less than Good Press.

When I sit down in one of the armchairs, I already feel the overwhelming urge to get out of the office. I don't really want to be here. Brian was right about it being a Saturday—last night, when I went off to do the 'hit,' I spent a long time thinking about how I would spend today, after the football match. To my mind, I'd imagined myself in bed, all tucked up, with only Lizzie for company.

"So, girls," Brian says, beaming as he takes his place on the sofa, eyeing Amy for surely much longer than is necessary, "I see that you've had a chance to meet—at least in this *new* context."

I exchange glances with Amy, sitting in the armchair opposite me.

We share a mutually vacuous smile.

"Now," Brian says, thrusting a finger up in the air, and launching himself up off his seat—Brian was never any good at staying still. Whisky still slopping about inside the glass tumbler, he ventures over to his drinks cabinet, paws through a few of the drawers, and then produces a pair of files. Just like the hit from the night before, the envelopes are brown, an A4-size. He dishes out one to me, and the other to Amy.

The two of us exchange glances once more before setting about opening our respective envelopes. Inside, I find all the standard hallmarks of the 'intelligence pack:'

Location of target.

Brief explanation of security.

Extraction plan.

I glance back up over the sheets of paper, look to Brian, who's back perching on the edge of the sofa, clutching his tumbler of whisky as if someone might be about to swipe it from him. "So," he says, a slight smile bringing out the crow's feet surrounding his eyes, "what'd you think?"

"Is this hit *real?*" I said. "I mean, this isn't your idea of another blind date?"

Brian takes a sip of whisky, sets the tumbler down on the coffee table with a slight *chink* of glass on glass. He clasps his hands together and leans forward, somewhat conspiratorially. "Anna," he says, "I'm sorry for last night." He slips a sidelong glance to Amy. "Just a bit of fun and games, eh?"

I feel my stomach sink just a little . . . all right *a lot*, at the thought that Amy and Brian might be 'banging.'

Brian returns his attention to me. "You're going to be working together on this hit."

"Why?" I blurt out.

Brian glances to Amy again, smiles lightly, then he turns to me once more. "Because, Anna," he says, "I told you so."

I breathe in deeply, look back down at the intelligence pack, then heave out a long and satisfying sigh. "Guess I'll have to cancel my date then . . ."

Chapter Seven

THAT WAS THE OTHER THING, at Ben's football match, right as we were on the point of leaving, I noticed Nathan's father—*Mark*—looming out of the corner of my eye. I know that I should've just swept Ben on into the car, not so much as looked back, and yet something deep inside me tugged hard. So hard that I couldn't resist.

Could it have been *desperation* for company?

Really, at thirty-six?

Seeing those round, sexy, hazel eyes of Mark's, I decided that there was no time like the present, and, with Nathan and Ben somewhat distracted, I asked if he'd like to, maybe, you know, go out for a drink sometime.

Well, 'sometime' turned out to be this evening.

Mark, as he explained, was in the habit of hiring a babysitter on Saturday nights so that he could go out to the cinema, visit a café with a good book . . . you know, do all the things that being a single parent don't allow you to do.

And though I'd already felt those first pangs of regret, of having to actually go through with the date—what am I *fourteen?* —I decided that, since I'd gone and asked, there was nothing else for me to do.

On the way out of Brian's office, I realised that there was *no way* I was going to call up Mark and cancel our 'date' just because I needed to go through with a hit later on . . . in any case, it wouldn't be until the early hours of the morning.

And it's not like I'm *that* sort of girl.

I agreed a meeting time with Amy, in the same moment feeling a little bit of regret seeping in, that little voice telling me that I was going to have to do some *babysitting* tonight myself . . . then again, I suppose that Amy *did* manage to point a gun at me last night.

Perhaps *I'm* the one to be babysat.

Is that the message Brian is trying to send?

Brian *does* have a habit of sending messages . . .

When I reach my front door, I can already tell that something's not right. It's nothing in particular—not like I tape a hair to the crack so I can see whether or not someone's been in or out of my house . . . though, maybe, in retrospect, I *should* start doing that . . . no, it's just a *sensation*, almost like a crawling sensation, just beneath the surface of my skin.

I slip my key into the lock, turn it, and hear the prongs—or whatever their technical name is—turning in the mechanism. There's a gentle *click* of the latch leaving its nook, and I slip in through the gap I've created.

I glance down to the floor of the hallway, to the loose tile in the corner, where I stash an emergency weapon—nothing major; just a little .32 calibre pistol—in the floor space.

Keeping my eye on the corridor to the kitchen, to the staircase leading up to my bedroom, I crouch down and run my hand over the tile. Find the edge. Lever my fingernails in around the crack. Prise it up. Still keeping my eyes on the area surrounding me, I pad about inside the space, expecting to feel the cool metal casing of the pistol.

But I feel nothing.

I'm so surprised that I continue to shove my hand into the gap—trying to see just into which nook it's ended up.

The truth is, though, that it's not there.

I straighten up, glance around, see Lizzie emerge from the kitchen doorway.

She stretches out her legs, lets loose a tiny *miaow* of greeting, and then struts up to me. She rubs her furry body against my side as I replace the tile.

I must've only turned my back for a second, but that was all it took.

"Think this's the second time in twenty-four hours you've been held at gunpoint."

My blood cools.

My brain kicks back into gear.

I give a slight shake of my head, and look off along the corridor.

Adam Alderknot.

AA to his friends . . . or whatever *I* am to him.

A fellow assassin.

"News gets around quickly," I say, rising to a standing position.

Eyeing my own gun which AA holds on me.

I take in AA's high cheekbones. His *spindly* body.

A shame that he's not interested in women.

Or, perhaps, knowing AA's personality as I do, maybe it's for the best . . .

Today he's wearing a black turtleneck sweater, black jeans, and ankle-high *spotless* boots. He looks a little like he's just emerged off a catwalk where the theme is 'burglar chic.'

What's most striking, though, is that he's grown his black hair out a little more at the top, and he's had a close shave around the sides.

"You look like a monk," I say. "All that's left is to cut a little circle in the middle of your scalp."

AA scoffs, then, clicking on the safety, tosses the pistol to me.

I catch it.

Then replace it where it once was.

"Like *you're* anyone to talk about fashion," he says, apparently paying an underhanded compliment to my trouser suit. He jerks his head in the direction of the kitchen. "Cup of tea?"

———

There's a lot that can be said about AA, and one of those things is that he knows how to make a *mean* cup of tea. I don't know quite what he does—maybe it has to do with dunking the teabags, allowing them to *brew* . . . I don't have the patience for crap like that.

So, while he prepares the tea, I set about finding a new hiding place for my gun—somewhere AA won't *immediately* uncover it.

When I sit myself back down at the kitchen table, I watch him tread across the room to the flip-top bin, a pair of steaming teabags perched on a single teaspoon. By some minor miracle, he doesn't spill a single drop on the kitchen floor.

Maybe he's a witch.

That'd explain a lot.

He brings over my cup of tea, sets his own down in front of him on my well-battered, once-lacquered cedar table top. "You look like shit," he says, as if that's *any* way to open a conversation.

I take a sip of my tea, and it's *delicious*. Thick, and milky, and with just a tiny spoonful of sugar. My tongue seems to quiver with gratitude . . . or something like it.

"So, have you come here to tell me about this young upstart?"

AA knocks back the entirety of his tea in one long swig—I wonder if he made his a little 'Irish.' Next, he crosses his legs one way, then the other, before fiddling with the edge of the table, a smirk sneaking onto his lips. "Not got any idea what you're talking about."

"Amy," I say, not feeling like playing this game—after all, I've got a packed evening: date followed by murder. "Amy Douglas," I add, as if it might help clear things up for him.

" 'Amy Douglas,' " he mouths back at me, as if he's attempting to pluck up the courage to speak some word in a foreign language.

I look back down into the mulchy-brown liquid—my cup of tea still a good three-quarters full. I've always been the type who likes to *savour* the little luxuries in life; I get no joy out of knocking them back the way that AA seems to prefer.

AA's eyes bob about the edge of the table for another few moments, and then, without warning, sneak up onto mine. That smirk of his gets so wide that I feel a strong urge to knock it all the way back down his throat. But I hold back. Tell myself that it *certainly would not* be ladylike.

"Yeah," AA says, a slight sigh to the tone of his voice, as if he's disappointed I'm not going to play the game. He stares down into his drained cup of tea, no doubt thinking about preparing another one . . . maybe it's just some elaborate ploy to conceal his drinking habits from me, as if *I* care . . . "I've come here about Amy," AA adds.

"So?" I say, taking another sip of tea. "What's the deal?"

"Amy Douglas," AA says, leaning back in his chair, folding his hands behind his head. "Amy. Doug-*luss.*"

I look at my wristwatch. "Just get on with it, won't you? You break into my home, hold me at *gunpoint,* if I wanted I could have you in a prison cell within the next five minutes."

AA beams back at me. "That's just the point, though, isn't it? I mean—*Amy Douglas*—she's all there is keeping us out of prison."

"What're you talking about?" I say, feeling a touch despondent now, having to admit to myself that AA knows more about the politics going on here than I do.

"Well," AA continues, clearly enjoying this power he holds over me, "Amy Douglas is the daughter of the Chief Constable of Police, I'll have you know."

"Yeah," I say, with the flicker of a smile, "already knew that."

AA closes one eye, gives me a mean look. "Right," he says, trying hard to make out he's unperturbed when he—*quite clearly*—is. "Well, do you also realise that Charles Branwick—"

"I believe he goes by *Charlie,* even in a professional capacity."

"Might as well just shut my mouth now and stop making a dick of myself, huh?"

I roll my eyes at him and then sip another millilitre of tea. "Go on," I say.

AA pauses for a long moment, no doubt trying to build up some sort of dramatic tension.

Then he continues.

"*Charlie* Branwick and Brian Mathewson, they're, what's the expression, *thick as thieves*."

"Uh huh," I answer him, though stop short of telling him that I knew *this* too . . . I can sense that AA's just getting to the good bit, the bit which I *don't* know about, and if there's anything I've learned about this particular job, it's never a good idea to broadcast the extent of one's ignorance.

"To put it bluntly," AA goes on, "Charlie Branwick is the one who's turning a blind eye whenever these hits happen, whenever there needs to be someone to put a hand on a Detective Inspector's shoulder and tell them to look the other way."

"Brian's safety net," I put in.

AA clicks his fingers at me, like an overenthusiastic trainee teacher. "*Exactly!*" he says.

I stare hard at the tiles above the kitchen counter, noticing that there's quite a large spot of mould growing there. I think about scrubbing it off, then wonder if it'd be overkill to hire a cleaner to take care of it . . . then I remind myself that, considering the amount of illegally held weapons I have concealed about the house, the last thing I should be doing is hiring help: especially the type of help that tends to get into all the nooks and crannies.

I look back to AA.

He goes on.

"And Amy, she was, well, Charlie's eyes on the ground—the one with the full picture, on just what was going on between Brian and Charlie. The problem is, though, that Amy, she started to get a little"—AA makes a revolver of his fingers, points it at me and squeezes the trigger—"you know?" he adds.

I think back to the first time I saw Amy—I think about the case that we worked together, *months ago now*. We had been tying up loose ends for Brian, keeping the profile of one of his clients clean—covering up the murder of his wife—and then, at the end, when we'd needed to let the matter lie, simply walk away, Amy had been unable to do so.

Her sense of justice had told her that Brian's client needed to die.

And so she did it.

With my own gun.

From what AA's saying, it sounds like that wasn't the last time that Amy took the law into her own hands, with the knowledge that her daddy would watch her back.

"And there was me," I say, "thinking that she wanted to make it on her own—all that business about changing her surname, using her mother's maiden name, or whatever . . . you think that was just a hollow gesture, nothing to it at all? She was prepared for her father to cover her tracks whatever she decided to do?"

"I dunno," AA says, glancing back over his shoulder to the kettle, "I'm a hired killer, not a detective."

———

Me and AA talk for about another half an hour, during which time—and I have *no* idea how he manages it—AA drags not only the information surrounding the hit for tonight, the one I'm doing with Amy, but also that I've got a date set-up for just before.

As I accompany AA to the front door of my house, we end up getting down into the topic of Amy Douglas once more. I look to AA, and say, "The way she was talking last night—how she was all hopped up, doing all this kind of puffing-her-chest-out crap, it sounded like she's lost that moral compass of hers; the one which led her into 'doing the right thing.'

"Yeah," AA says, resting his fingers on the latch to the front door, "I suppose that once you see what sort of money's involved in this game, it does a good trick of greasing up *anybody's* moral compass."

"Even so," I continue, "something about it seems *off* . . . I mean, with Amy Douglas, you really think that her dad kicked her off the Force?"

AA shrugs. "Amy's daddy's gotta answer to someone, even if it is the Prime Minister, and maybe they got tired of having to be responsible for Charlie's daughter's bad-girl act."

"Sounds plausible," I reply.

AA depresses the latch on the front door. He glances back over my shoulder, back to the staircase. I wonder if he's just seen Lizzie slink out of the hiding place in the airing cupboard . . . where she *always* goes whenever there're strangers in the house.

But instead of making some nauseating sound at my cat, AA just nods to the third step up on the staircase. "I can see where you've stashed the gun from here." He glances back at me, gives me another one of his trademark smirks, then says, "Take care, Anna, it's not a toy."

I think of telling AA about the diary—about what Amy handed me the night before—but I decide, for two reasons, not to say a word. One, it'd be just another opportunity for him to goad me about my out-of-the-loopness, and, two, he'd no doubt snatch it away from me, saying something along the lines of 'let the big boys play with fire.'

Well, I'm a Big Girl now.

And I think I can handle myself just fine around fire.

As AA slips around the front door, I manage to get a hard slap on his right buttock.

That'll teach him.

Sometimes I wonder if what AA needs is a little discipline.

Someone to show *him* who's boss.

Chapter Eight

I TAKE GREAT PAINS to get myself ready, and my cat Lizzie plays the female confidante, crouched on the foot of my bed—on top of the scrunched-up duvet—furrowing her brow at, seemingly, every one of the choices which I make:

First I go for gold earrings, and then silver ones.

Finally, I settle for sapphire, but then that makes my complexion look washed out.

I stand before the full-length mirror, hearing the throbbing beats of hip-hop music pounding outside my window, emanating from one of my dear neighbour's homes. I've been thinking about moving—been thinking about getting out of this neighbourhood, it's hardly true that I really *need* to be here any longer. In the course of the past year, or so, Brian seems to have become somewhat happier about us assassins not keeping such a low profile. AA—for *Christ's sake*—has moved himself into a four-bedroom flat in Kensington.

Mr Inconspicuous.

As for me, though, I have to admit that it's not all about what Brian wants.

One of the most important things to keep in mind is my *own* safety.

The safety of my *family*:

Of Ben, and my daughter Josie; my ex-husband, Arnold, and —*yes*—even Arnold's new partner *Kate*.

Living here, in this area of the city, I'm not likely to have to answer the question of what I do for a living . . . if the neighbours even speak to me at all.

Because gossip can be a real killer:

Brian just takes it to the next level.

In the end, I settle on a V-necked blouse over the top of a pair of snug-fitting jeans. I slip on a sensible, beige jacket over the top—one of those that I bought sometime, from *somewhere*, but haven't ever had an occasion to use it for.

When I inspect myself in the mirror, I think that I look borderline prepared for a night out . . . the diamond earrings and necklace seem to make up for the rest of my garb.

I slip on a pair of flat-soled shoes—*black, of course*—and then I get myself all set for the second event of my evening: the hit that'll take place a bit later.

Apparently having cottoned onto the fact that I'm going out for the evening—and wishing to state her position on this matter —Lizzie rises up on the bed, arches her back, and waits for me to stroke her back. I do as she wishes, and listen to her give a sustained *purr*.

"Be back later," I say to her, heading out the door of my bedroom, clicking off the light switch as I go.

———

Earlier, Mark sent me the details for a restaurant where we should meet.

I walk along with my mobile phone squeezed in my paw, a little too much like those reams of tourists, which cling to the streets of London day and night, for my liking.

There's a touch of frost in the air tonight, and I can feel the chill cutting me right down to the bone. I'm glad that I had the presence of mind to grab and overcoat off the hook as I rushed on out through my front door.

I pick out the place, an Italian:

Ranielli's

The sign is written out in a florid script, perhaps supposed to reflect spaghetti, something like that—I don't *really* know; I've never been that artistically minded.

As I approach the door to the restaurant, I notice that all the windows are steamed-up, and that the place is filled with the shadowy forms of diners within. I can make out the flurrying orange flicker of candlelight inside, too, and I can't help thinking that me and Mark might just be of the same heart.

We like our basic, no-frills food in a *vaguely* romantic setting.

All of a sudden, I feel just a touch underdressed.

No time to worry about that, though, because, before I've so much as caught my bearings completely, I hear Mark's, now-familiar, voice on my heels.

"Anna," he says, his voice much thicker, a touch gruffer than I recall.

I turn to him, see him standing there.

He's ditched his oilskin overcoat, and now wears a sensible, well-cut, black jacket, over the top of a crisp, white shirt and a pair of jeans. He wears a pair of nicely polished shoes underneath, too. He has hoiked his shoulder-length hair back into a ponytail, and it doesn't look seedy at all . . . I wonder—briefly—how he managed to pull *that* off.

His appearance, as pleasant as it *is*, isn't exactly what draws my attention, though.

I see that he's holding something in his hands.

When I squint a touch—maybe Brian's driver was right about me needing glasses—I make out the object he holds in his hands.

A miniature, wood-carved rocking chair.

With a smile, he hands it over to me. "Just as promised," he says.

For a few seconds, I stand there stunned. I recall how he said he was going to make a chair for my cat. And even though the rocking chair is clearly too small for a cat of Lizzie's bulk, I can see past this deficiency.

I look up into those rich, beautifully hazel eyes of his. This just might be the most romantic thing that *anybody* has done for me.

Ever.

It starts as a tingling feeling down deep in my gut, and then, before I can control it, it works its way up through me.

To my brain.

And I can't control it anymore.

I lean up into Mark's face, into his thick features, his *strong* features, and I press my lips up against his. He's as taken aback as I am for several moments. Like some fifteen-year-old boy, he doesn't know what to do. Before I can help myself, I reach my hand up around his back, and to the tip of his ponytail . . . just about as high as I can reach when he stands up straight.

He smells of sawdust and cologne. I can feel his heart beating hard against my chest; can *hear* his heart beating beneath his skin. His breath tastes of a combination of coffee and toothpaste.

In the end, it's Mark who pulls back from me, his eyes round, and wide, and his lips slightly parted in shock . . . *good* shock, I hope.

He runs his fingers over his hair and tugs at his ponytail. Then he breaks out into a smile. "I . . . I really *like* you, Anna," he says.

I arch an eyebrow, place a hand on my hip. "Well, I really like *you* too, Mark."

————

A black-haired, Italian-accented waiter seats us over in the corner of the restaurant, where a flickering candle is set—in that rustic style—into the neck of a drained bottle of wine.

It stands in the middle of a white table cloth.

Mark—the gentleman that he clearly is—slips around to pull out the chair for me, and I sit down. He takes up the seat opposite me, and, for a long few seconds, the two of us just stare into one another's eyes . . . all *lovey-dovey*.

The waiter breaks off this tender moment by handing us each a leather-bound menu. As I peruse the options within, the text kept nice and snug on its laminated page, I can't help but notice the meatballs that've just arrived at the table beside our own.

I look over the grey-haired couple, see how the two of them —with their leathered skin—still gaze adoringly across the table at one another. I watch on as the couple clink their glasses of red wine together across the table, and then, never breaking eye contact, take a sip.

Could that be me and Mark?

I try to flush that thought from my brain as soon as it enters.

If there's anything that *screams*, 'terminal cat lady,' then that stream of thought is surely it . . .

I turn my attention back to the options on offer, and, in the end, go with chicken alfredo with fettuccine, while Mark goes for some fishy dish—I suppose that he didn't get the memo, the Top Tips for a First Date:

Number One: Steer Clear of Fish Breath.

Then again, considering his timidity from our impromptu first kiss outside the restaurant, I can't help but feel that he, perhaps, has no more kissing in mind for tonight.

Much less anything *further*.

Neither of us orders wine—perhaps Mark *really is* the One— and we talk about superficial things. When the talk turns to our respective sons, I'm a little ashamed about not being able to pitch in as much as Mark.

The obvious, unspoken truth is that, quite plainly, I really don't know all that much about Ben at all. In the end, I manage to scrape up some sort of comment about how Ben spends all day 'glued' to his videogames, and that seems to see me through on some basic level.

As we await our dessert—for me: a chocolate tart; for Mark: an orange sorbet—I turn my attention to the ornamental little rocking chair that he carved for me earlier in the day.

I have little knowledge of anything vaguely practical so really have no idea of the sort of work involved in creating such a thing. But, at least to my eye, the fact that all the corners seem to have been nicely sanded down, and that the cut of the wood is totally smooth to the touch, I suppose that Mark *did* take a good amount of his Saturday afternoon in making it for me.

I glance up at him, seeing that he's taking a sip of water,

looking around the restaurant, no doubt still feeling somewhat nervous about this whole experience.

And I can't help but feel the *sweetness* purging from the pores in his skin.

"Is this the sort of thing you work on?" I say.

Mark locks his eyes back onto mine. He gives a slight smile. "Usually they're a little bigger than that—I take on commissioned work, *bespoke* pieces, mainly."

"And that pays the bills, does it?"

His thicker smile tells me that it *certainly* does . . . and then some.

The perennial question comes when Mark sets his water glass back down on the table. When he clears his throat a touch, meets my eye, and says, "So, Anna, what do you do for a living?"

Chapter Nine

A S CHILLY AS THE AIR was a few hours ago, when I walked back from the restaurant with Mark, it's now reached a whole other level. I can hardly keep my teeth from chattering together, despite the thick, black fleece; the leather gloves; a balaclava; and thermal underwear I have on.

I feel the weight of *Punisher* holstered into the back of my belt.

I do my best to keep the light from the torch steady on the door handle, shining it so that Amy can see what she's doing.

We're way out in the countryside—a good hour's drive out of the city to get here.

In the near distance, over the rolling hills which surround this country estate, I can hear a couple of sheep bleating; the odd horse snorting; here and there a *moo* from a cow.

No dogs, yet, though.

That's the important thing.

The air reeks of manure and freshly fallen rain.

I suppose that's *one* thing to be thankful for, that it hasn't rained tonight.

Working on a Saturday night is all about the small victories . . .

"Anna?" Amy says, her voice just above a whisper. She tilts her head slightly back towards me. "Can you keep the torch still?"

"Sorry," I say, realising that I've allowed the tiny circle of light to drift off across the wall.

We parked the car up about fifteen minutes' walk away.

Down an inconspicuous lane—or, at least, the plan was for the lane *to be* inconspicuous, whether it turns out that way, or not, remains to be seen . . .

On the walk here, neither of us could use a torch.

That would've just broadcast our whereabouts to anyone who happened to peer out of one of the upper-floor windows of the estate.

It's not like that many people come out here for a night-time stroll.

Not unless they're here on *business*.

Ivy snakes its way up the white plaster wall and Amy continues to work at the lock on the wooden door. In our information packs, we were given a very specific approach route for the estate: a route which would ensure we wouldn't get spotted on the way here. This exterior door—*apparently*—remains unseen by any security devices.

There's a metal *tinkle* as Amy drops the lock-picking kit.

"*Shit,*" she mutters, crouching down to search for it.

I shine the torch over the area Amy is searching.

The metal attachment of the lock-pick reflects the light.

"Want me to have a go?" I say.

Amy doesn't reply right away, and I take her non-reaction as a sign of petulance. However, when she eventually does straighten up, and looks back at me, I can see that she's frustrated with herself, that she has a whole series of frown lines engrained in her forehead.

"Here," she says, shoving the lock-pick at me.

I roll my eyes, without her seeing, and hand her over the torch.

I get the door open in a matter of seconds.

This doesn't seem to cheer Amy up at all.

In fact, Amy shoves by me, squeezes herself through the gap.

Has some kind of childish desire to be the *first*.

I wonder briefly about where professionalism went in this business, and then I follow her through the doorway.

———

Twice I need to grab hold of the back of Amy's jacket; realising that she's—*unwittingly*—about to step into the range of a camera with night-vision capabilities.

Amy seems to note these lapses in concentration, but, again, they're shown in the form of frowns, or the shaking of her head.

When she threatens to go and walk into the range of a camera for a third time, I decide that enough's enough, and I haul her into the wall of the estate, not worried about dirtying both of our boots with the soil from a flowerbed.

Sometimes you've just got to get your shoes dirty.

"Look," I say, in a hushed voice, "you're going to get both of us caught if you keep going like this. How about you let me lead the way for a while, huh?"

Amy gives me a steely glance. Then her lips twist in a smirk. "Just like when they got that helicopter out—*searching* for you?"

I feel my heart leap in my chest.

That was more than a year ago now . . . it seems so far in the past . . . and yet, at the same time, I know that in reality it wasn't.

I realise the point she's trying to make is that I'm just as fallible as she is, but that doesn't mean I appreciate her making it right now.

"Listen," I say, grabbing hold of Amy when I see that she's attempting to sneak off from me again, "you're all jumped up tonight—is there something you want to tell me?"

Amy's blue eyes appear almost transparent in the dark. Her smirk has disappeared from her lips now. "Did you read the diary?"

" 'The diary?' " I say, and then recall the leather-bound, burgundy pocket book which Amy handed me the night before. I shake my head. "I've had other stuff on my mind, believe it or not, a *packed* schedule." I grip Amy tight, feeling her muscles slacken just a little—a welcome change from how she was holding them all *rigid* tight just a few moments ago. "I tell you what," I say, "first thing tomorrow, I promise that I'll give it a read, okay? Will you put your mind to the task at hand now?"

Amy stares at me, long and hard, and then gives a nod.

"Good," I say, then turn my attention back to the house, looming above us. "Then let's get to work."

Right as I ready to let Amy go, I notice that grenade of hers strapped down onto her belt. I yank her back. "You brought that along?" I say. "*Why?*"

Amy shrugs at me, a slight pout on her lips. "Thought it might come in useful."

I give a shake of my head, think long and hard about ripping it right off her, tossing it away into one of the flowerbeds.

But I don't.

I just hope she won't get in my way.

————

Considering Amy's jumped-up state, I take the executive decision to guide us into the house itself.

It's not too tricky. There's a burglar alarm, but I disarm it quickly, with the help of a device I was given as part of the briefing. I take care of the mains power, too . . . a rookie error, if there ever was one, not to flip that off.

Inside the house, according to the intelligence pack, there're no cameras.

Usually a good indication of someone this uptight about *external* security having something to hide.

But it's also one less thing to think about.

I withdraw *Punisher* from its holster.

Hold it down at my side.

That makes me feel a little more confident.

A little more *in control.*

As the two of us skulk about the darkened interior of the house, I can't help but feel on edge . . . not because I'm potentially about to kill someone—that's the *easiest* part of any hit—but because I've got this hot young thing on my heels; and no way of predicting what she's going to do next.

Moonlight beams in through the windows of the kitchen, and I catch sight of a pile of plates—all of them dirty, and left stacked on the counter. The air smells of leftover food—lasagne?

I wonder if it's the housekeeper's weekend off . . . or maybe they're that *humble* kind of rich—the kind that doesn't have a problem stacking their own dishes in the dishwasher.

"Anna?" Amy says, out of the darkness behind me.

"What?" I say, a little annoyed, and wishing that she'd just shut her trap for the duration of the job.

"Can I, you know, *do* it?"

I hold myself still, push my back up against the wall of the kitchen. I feel the slight chill of a tile against the back of my neck. I'm in no mood to be having this conversation, and yet, at the same time, I want Amy to calm the *hell* down.

I look to her, give a slight, almost imperceptible nod.

Amy nods back at me, her expression the same.

I lead us onwards, up a narrow flight of stairs which was clearly designed—from a couple of centuries ago—to be utilised by the house staff . . . but which, *tonight*, will be used by a pair of Angels of Death.

When we reach the top of the staircase, my eyes flit to the shadows. I operate on instinct. Scoping out the place for any sign of a threat. Seeing nothing at all, I gesture for Amy to step forwards, to follow after me.

I feel my heart beating hard against my throat as the two of us keep flush to the wall of the corridor. At the edge of my consciousness, I'm aware of Amy preparing her gun. Getting ready to take the scalp which she—*apparently*—so badly needs.

Once again, I curse Brian, and whatever it is he's up to.

Just what *is* he trying to pull?

When we reach the door to the master bedroom, I look to Amy, give her a nod.

This is where the target will be hiding out.

Alone . . . if the intelligence pack is to be believed.

Amy gives me another long, lingering glance—one of those

looks which tells me, in no uncertain terms, that I should probably be the one doing the steady-hand work here . . . but I
already promised her, and there's no telling what little thing it'll
take to push her over the edge.

She reaches out for the door handle, I grip my gun tighter,
hold it down at my side, pointed to the floorboards at my feet. I
allow my finger to hover over the trigger.

My heart thumps once.

Twice.

A third time.

Amy opens up the door.

A low-level *growl* sounds.

And then, with a *yelp*, this large black bundle leaps out of the
darkness.

Chapter Ten

MY EYE IS IN.

I line up the shot.

But I hesitate.

Just long enough for the dog—some kind of *enormous*, long-haired, black mongrel—to take a chunk out of Amy's throat.

With a suppressed *whistle*, a bullet flies through the air.

Brings the dog down with a final, dead *thunk*.

Making a gasping sound, gulping for breath in spite of the departing blood, Amy pads about her, pads the floorboards.

Seeing that she's dropped her gun, and that it's landed down at the toe of my boot, I stoop for it. I clench hold of it moments before Amy's hand gets there.

She holds her other hand to her throat.

Blood dribbles down her neck in the moonlight.

Drips at her feet.

I think about what I've done, about how I *had* the chance to take the dog down.

That if I'd only acted quicker—acted on *instinct*—the dog never would've got so much as its snout up against Amy's skin.

But I didn't.

I held off.

I *wanted* the dog to bite Amy.

To teach her a lesson?

". . . Anna," Amy hisses at me, "*Anna!*"

From the half-open door of the bedroom, I can hear a constant *click-click-click*.

The target—no doubt—attempting to switch on their bedside light.

And having no luck at all.

There's no time here.

Amy remains in my face. "*Anna,*" she says, "*Anna!*"

I shove her to one side, my mind still filled to the brim with what I've done.

Wondering whether Amy—too—realises what I've done.

Before I leave her alone, I grab hold of the grenade that clips onto her belt, glad now that she's brought it along to tonight's hit.

My gun squeezed tightly in my grip, Amy's stuck in the back of the waistband of my trousers, I slip into the bedroom.

I skulk about the darkness.

See the form rising up off the bed.

I grip hold of the grenade, rip the tab free.

Toss it.

Sure enough, smoke spurts up from within.

Smothers *everything*.

It stinks of sulphur.

Fills my eyes; my airways.

But I keep my mind on the target.

This time I don't hesitate.

I squeeze the trigger.

Just like the dog, the target drops to the floor with a percussive *thump*.

Life gone.

Mission complete.

I turn my back on the target, slumped beneath the cloud of smoke, then return to Amy, outside the bedroom.

Amy stares down at the crumpled form of the dead dog as smoke begins to seep out from the master bedroom.

I take a moment to analyse the dog's bloodied jaws.

The type of dog that's been trained to bite.

I see that it's missing fur, here and there.

Although I was never an animal person, I feel pity for the creature.

And yet think that this is—*most likely*—for the better.

If I had left the dog alive, it might've jumped out and attacked one of the police officers who will soon arrive to the premises.

The net result would've been the same.

Perhaps it would've been crueller.

I grab hold of the dazed Amy, still bleeding all over the place, and I shove her before me.

I know that I can show no sympathy.

Because showing sympathy can indicate *guilt*.

And there's nothing I should feel guilty about.

———

We're about halfway back to the car before I pay attention to Amy, to the way she keeps constantly repeating my name. As if it was some sort of mantra. Once I've got off the phone to Brian, to tell him that we'll need a clean-up crew on the scene before the police are called in, I stop Amy dead in the middle of the road, and say, "You thought this was all so easy, didn't you? Just a *fun* game for you to play?" I can feel a touch of bile twist in my stomach. "But, you know what, your daddy can't protect you everywhere, and there's a limit to his power. What do you think would've happened if they'd found your blood back there—on the scene, huh?"

Amy's eyes are glassy, they seem almost hollow.

Her complexion is pale and I can tell that she's not a thousand miles off fainting.

I whip off my balaclava and she uses it to apply pressure to the bite marks on her throat.

I grab hold of her again, shove her into the road ahead. "Come on," I say, "let's get you home to Daddy."

I lay Amy down on the back seat of the car from the Mathewson Media carpool: one of the many, utterly anonymous, second-hand hatchbacks which Brian keeps. As I grip the steering wheel, I wonder where he gets his stock of them from. Does Brian have a specific dealer who calls him up whenever 'One Lady Owner' walks into the showroom?

I can still taste the cheese from my meal earlier at the back of my throat, although the dinner with Mark seems about a thousand years ago. I think about the question he asked me—the question that I've been asked *so many times* . . . and I recall what I told him.

The truth.

How I said to him—*no bullshit*—that I'm a hired assassin for a publicist.

I thought that he would laugh.

Or run.

But he did neither.

He just stayed calm, smiled vaguely and said, in a mysterious sort of a way, "We've all got secrets, haven't we? Skeletons at the backs of our closets?"

That one moment in the dinner sent a flare up my spine.

I can still feel it now, driving away from the target's house.

Away from the mission me and Amy have just completed.

Just what did he mean by it?

I'd half expected, following my admission, and his cryptic reply, that he would grab me by the hand and lead me off down some side alley. That he'd whip my trousers down and have me up against a brick wall.

But that wasn't what happened at all.

We split the bill, and he gave me a kiss—*on the cheek*—at the door of the restaurant.

Then the two of us slipped away.

Into the night.

He left me wondering if that 'ornamental carpentry' day job of his is just that . . . if he has a secret equally as devious as my own.

———

Once I drop Amy off at an approved care point—a couple of paramedics approaching the car at the private clinic Brian sent me to—I drive the car back to the carpool at Mathewson Media.

Instead of going home, though, I decide to take the lift up to the thirteenth floor.

In all truth—given that I'm still armed, that *Punisher* is still holstered at my belt—I expect someone to stop me . . . I think that, at the very least, a member of security might pop up out of the shadows, demand that I get down.

But, no.

Nobody at all.

I wonder if it's because Brian trusts me.

. . . Or if there's some other reason.

When I get to the enormous, ornately carved walnut doors of Brian's office, I rap my knuckles and wait for a reply. I can see the fuzzy, orange glow of electric light seeping out from the crack at the base of the door. I know that Brian's in the office.

He's *always* in the office.

Sometimes I wonder if the man sleeps.

There's a gentle *murmur* from within, and I take it as my cue to slip inside.

Once again, I glance back over my shoulder, sure that someone—*some* member of security—must be following on my heels.

But there's no one that I can see.

Brian's office reeks of the same woody joss-stick scent from the day before. It tickles the back of my throat, and brings a sneeze to the very tip of my nose. Somehow I hold off. Maybe my body realises the importance of the meeting here.

The *gravity* of the thing.

Brian's sitting in one of the armchairs, the back of it turned to me, and I can see the waft of cigar smoke rising up. Now that I think of it, I can smell the cigar smoke mingling with the scent of the woody joss stick. He has a lamp beside him clicked on—the only light in the room.

It has the effect of making it seem like Brian is the *centre* of the room.

Just how he likes it, I suppose.

In keeping with the majesty of his office.

"Brian?" I say.

I wait for an answer.

I see his shirt sleeve, Brian's elbow, on the armrest of the chair. I hear a slight *tinkle* of ice in a tumbler just beyond, out of sight from where I stand.

"I want to talk," I say.

I wait for a long few moments, wondering if Brian has maybe slipped off to Dreamland. If his acknowledgement for me to enter was actually just him talking in his sleep.

But then comes his reply.

". . . Anna?" he says.

I take this as my permission to approach His Majesty.

I round the armchair, look down at him.

Brian's slumped low in the armchair, his tumbler of whisky clutched to his stomach. He's wearing a cream shirt with purple pinstripes. The sleeves are rolled up. Dark bags cling to the bases of his eye sockets and each cheek has a deep pit embedded in it. His dark-brown, dyed hair is all out of place, sticking up in tufts, exposing the white, flaking skin of his scalp.

I catch a slight whiff of body odour; a large dose of cologne administered in a vain attempt to cover it up.

On the glass coffee table, I eye the ashtray, where Brian has left his cigar, precariously balancing between the notches in the ceramic mould.

Brian's eyes seem to be out of focus. He doesn't look at me. He stares out through the window of his office—to the street outside. Finally, when I'm on the point of getting down in his face and grabbing him by the neck of his shirt, he responds.

Unable to so much as keep his head straight on his neck, he stares up at me.

When he speaks his voice is nothing more than a cracked whisper. "I'm so sorry, *Anna*." His voice rasps in his throat. "A big mistake."

If I have one weakness, it's my patience.

Even when faced with someone who—quite *rightly*; employer or not—deserves a reprimand for their actions, I, more often than not, find that I'm not capable of delivering said reprimand. I always wait for an explanation.

For a *lie*.

For *something*.

I cross my arms over my chest, and then, calm, cool, ask him, "Why?"

Brian smiles to himself, as if this is some sort of a joke. His eyes are *swimming* in their sockets and I can't help thinking to myself that, if somebody wished to take care of Brian Mathewson, then this would be the perfect time to do it. He's out of his wits—there's no security coming . . . if I wanted to . . . if I could just . . . I might be able to do it—*right now*.

"Anna?" Brian says, breaking off my train of thought.

"Yes?" I reply.

"Why do you continue to work for me?"

I hold myself still, prepare the standard answer. "I want my kids to have a good future—I don't want to be a bad mother anymore."

Brian winces, as if I've slipped the blade of a knife beneath one of his gnarled fingernails. "No," he replies, "No, I don't think that's the reason." Once more, he turns his head, almost performing the action in slow motion. Hand shaking, he sets his tumbler down on the glass coffee table. He holds a finger out to me, as if accusing me of something. "There's something deeper —something that you're not *telling* me." He shakes his head. "It's not the money, I've done the sums, you've got enough money for your kids. Enough money to tide you over."

I feel a smile tweak its way onto my lips.

It's true in the past year or so I've really cleaned up with Mathewson Media.

And I still have the majority of it.

I never was a big spender.

I allow myself a sigh. I watch as my breath steams up the window, and then look through the clouded-up glass, down to the street below. To the few passing black cabs at this time; their orange lights lit up.

"You're afraid," Brian says, his voice now much clearer, none of the gruffness which accompanied it only moments before.

I look down at him.

Somehow, he seems to have grown in stature, just from sitting in that armchair.

He perches on the edge of the cushion now, eyeing me closely.

"You went away, you thought about it," he says, "and you came back to me, having made the decision . . . a decision that you've stuck by for a sizeable chunk of time now. I notice, too, that you've stopped going to see that therapist of yours." He pauses for the longest time, then adds, "Julie."

I hold my breath right down at the base of my lungs.

For some reason, it becomes almost impossibly difficult for me to breathe out.

Some dizzy speculations pass through my brain.

That Brian has—*somehow*—masterminded me to come here, to his office, tonight, so that he might kill the killer.

But, first things first . . . he wants to *humiliate* me, and *then* kill me.

I breathe out.

Bring the scene clear again.

Remind myself who's *who* here.

Who should be answering the questions.

I give a slight shake of my head, look back to Brian. "I'm not working with Amy again—she's an amateur."

Brian sits back in his armchair. He clasps his hands, then holds them in his lap.

"She almost got both of us killed," I add.

Brian pouts slightly, tilts his head to one side. "Extremely fierce dog, was it?"

I glare back at him, think about the dog.

It *was* fierce.

"Do you know what I think, Anna?" Brian says, glancing back out the window of his office.

"What?"

"I think that you *let* that dog bite Amy."

I feel a chilly sensation enter my blood.

My heart skips several beats.

I have a prickling feeling over the surface of my skin.

"Oh," Brian continues, "I have no proof—nothing like that—it's just a hunch." He glances back at me, eyebrows raised. "Hot or cold?"

I break off eye contact with him, unwilling to give him the pleasure. "She doesn't know what she's doing," I go on, "she crumples beneath pressure—you should've seen her trying to pick the lock on the exterior door, something that a teenager with his first kit wouldn't have trouble with."

"You were like that once," Brian says.

The body odour, the woody scent of the joss stick, and the smell of the cigar smoke becomes too much for me to bear. A crippling nausea squeezes in on my stomach. I stare at the dead cigar—no longer than a thumb now, and having gone out while we were speaking.

More than anything else I want to get out of Brian's office.

Get to some fresh air.

But, at the same time, I know that Brian won't let me leave.

Not yet.

Not without answering *one more* question.

And here it comes.

"You can walk away, Anna," Brian says, "any time you like."

He shifts his weight in his armchair.

His eyes meet mine.

"Just walk away."

Chapter Eleven

DESPITE HAVING STAYED UP late for the past couple of nights running, I find it impossible to sleep. The fact that Lizzie won't stop shoving her head up against me, wanting me to make a fuss of her, hardly helps me to get rest. In the end, I shut Lizzie out of my bedroom, bring my pillow down over my head, and then cry to myself.

For maybe half an hour.

That done, I shovel myself up and throw on my dressing gown—pilfered from some hotel, or other—over the tank top and cotton short shorts I wear to bed. I go to the bedroom door and see that Lizzie is sleeping there, her tortoiseshell fur moving in and out with her deep breathing.

Apparently unfazed by the earlier snub, she raises herself up from her slumber, and rubs her furry body against my exposed calf.

I tread past her and onto the landing.

I stand there for a minute or so; struck down with fatigue, and yet with no intention of returning to bed.

I force myself down the stairs to my kitchen where I dig out a bowl and a packet of cereal. A trickle of milk later and I sit at the table and plunge into my *impromptu* morning feast. I only begin to feel human again once I've boiled myself an instant coffee and—because it's something of a special occasion—I give Lizzie her breakfast early.

It's when I've just finished up washing my bowl and spoon, and I'm returning the spoon to its family, in its assigned drawer, that I stumble across the diary.

The leather-bound, burgundy pocket book with the gold-tipped pages.

Although my head throbs at the prospect of leafing it open, I force myself to do so.

I look over the first page, all that screwy, squiggly handwriting there.

Red ink.

In the harsh light of the kitchen, I force myself to make out the forms.

To give them sense in my brain.

And perhaps it's because I've had no sleep, that my brain is now working on a subconscious level, or maybe it's because I'm not having to contend with perpetual motion, like I did back in the car, but I have no trouble at all bringing the message clear:

To Mitsy,

Merry Christmas!

May your year be full of success and the very best of times!

Lots of love

BM

I look up from the diary, as if he might be standing in the doorway, keeping an eye on me while I look this diary over:
Brian Mathewson.

————

Thankfully, since the diary was intended for 'Mitsy,' the handwriting within isn't in Brian's near-illegible scrawl. The ink within —uniformly—is black, and although the writing is tight, I can easily make sense of it.

The year states that the diary is from twenty, twenty-five years ago.

The first pages—the ones with all the yearly planners, the contact details—are all blank.

I swear to myself silently, wishing that I might know just a little more about this 'Mitsy' before taking a stab at reading this diary.

Still, it's something which Amy wants me to read, and it's with that thought—the vague hope that I'll be able to understand her behaviour—that drives me on through the pages.

Although the diary is surely intended to be more of a practical device, I realise, after the first few entries, the first couple of weeks, that it turns away from such notes as: 'hair appointment 4 p.m.' or 'dentist's 11 a.m.' to far more detailed, more *illuminating* accounts.

Lizzie yowls at my feet, and I push back my kitchen chair just far enough so that she has space to leap up.

So, cat in lap, I set about reading Mitsy's diary.

————

21ˢᵗ January, 19—

Dearest, I never did thank you for giving me such a precious gift as this diary. It really was quite thoughtful of you. I have immediately been struck by the sheer practicality *of it, how my* unorganised, thoughtless *life now*—finally!—*has some sort of structure . . .*

Coming up for air, and a sip of my bitter, black coffee, I can't help but feel the stinging sarcasm almost spitting off the page.

Already, I have some leads:

Brian's wife?

Or some lover?

One of the two.

I read on:

. . . I suppose that, in a way, this little diary you thought to give me this Christmas was something of a wry joke, some sort of a comment, *about how I'm never seemingly happy with any of the gifts you present me with. But, well, the truth of the matter is that I* am *happy*—but happy because *I get to spend time with you. It seems, these days, that time with Brian Mathewson is a more valu-able commodity than* any *ruby or diamond a guy could buy a gal!*

Lizzie purrs away on my lap.

I can't help feeling just a little icky inside.

To be the one sitting here, at my kitchen table, early in the darkness of an October morning, reading what was—*surely*—supposed to be a private diary. Of course I have no guilt about 'betraying' Brian . . . he lives his life in the public domain, he makes a business of taking advantage of the private for profit and, often, *fun* . . . on the other hand, though, I do feel a little for this woman.

That said, it doesn't stop me from reading more.

As I peel back the pages, I can almost feel her loneliness rippling off the page.

The sarcasm dials down.

And the sense that this—this *diary*—acted as a sort of therapist for the poor woman begins to hit home.

Despite all that I've read so far, though, I struggle to see just why Amy chose to give the diary to me. I continue turning the pages, scanning now, trying to grasp what might be going on within the entries.

But I find nothing else of interest.

Only more outpourings of a lonely soul.

Someone with too much money; too little time.

When the sun peeps in through the kitchen windows, I give a long, hard yawn and then lay the book down on the table with a *slap* that wakes Lizzie.

I get up from the kitchen chair, lifting Lizzie up high in my arms, and then say to her, in a cutesy voice that would drive me *insane* to hear from somebody else, "Let's go get us some sleeple-weeple."

That poor cat.

Chapter Twelve

I N THE COURSE of the next week, I hear nothing at all from Brian.

I wonder if I've managed to wander into his bad books. I suppose, when he did finally sober up, he might've been a little concerned about the security breach at Mathewson Media . . . how a trained killer managed to steal right into his office, where he sat incapacitated.

I read on with the diary, leafing through a few pages whenever I have a spare moment here or there. But it all seems pretty much the same deal as what came before, until one page—about three or four from the end of the year.

One which has me flinching—Lizzie diving off my lap with a *hiss*—and almost has me spitting my tea out all over the little pocket book:

Today should've been a wonderful day. It should've been a time for celebration. But I couldn't find the strength to say anything at all

*about it. You see, I'm pregnant, at long last, though I know you took
every precaution for this not to happen. I've suspected as much for a
few months now, but I thought I'd just wait another week or so
before going to the doctor to confirm the inevitable. I suppose, on some
level, I thought that it might go away.*

Hoped it might go away.

*Having lived in your world for so long, I know that it is no place to
bring up a young child—let alone a daughter!—and so have taken
measures to leave.*
I won't bother you. I won't look for any sort of revenge.

I shall just be gone.

And you, Brian, dearest, will never even know you're the father.

I'm determined that's the way it will be.

I straighten up, stare out across the kitchen.
I blink several times, trying to bring the blurred shapes clear.
I really *do* need to get going with booking an eye test.
Before I think to myself any more, I reach for my mobile.
Call up AA.
Ask him over.

———

AA shows up within about twenty minutes—something which I
find a little disturbing. I can't help wondering if he's been parked
up in some alleyway nearby waiting for my call.

I barely have enough time to ditch my pyjama bottoms and tank top for a—*wholly more respectable, and almost stain-free*—white-blouse-and-jean combination.

A pair of sandals completes the look.

When AA arrives on my doorstep, his cheeks are a touch rosy. His black hair sticks up in tufts. Already, the sides of his hair look like they could do with a trim, if he wants to maintain that *haircut* of his.

I can smell the beer on his breath. "Great," I mutter, half to myself, "more drunks."

As AA prises his black leather jacket off and hangs it up on the coat rack in the hallway, he raises an explanatory finger to me. "Not drunk," he says, with a slight slur.

I roll my eyes as I lead him into the kitchen.

To the diary awaiting us on the table.

While I make the tea, I allow AA a free rein on the diary. I watch on from the kitchen counter, slipping him sidelong glances. He sits a little way forwards, perched on the edge of the chair, with his arms folded in front of him. For some reason, this sight tickles me and I can't help having a little giggle.

AA shifts a glance off in my direction, a smirk now lining his lips. "What's going on with you, Little Miss Chuckles?" And then, before I have a chance to wipe the shit-eating grin off my face, his eyes widen, and he glares at me with glee. He throws back the chair, leaps up to his feet and points hard at my chest, as if he was a townsperson, hundreds of years ago, pointing out a witch to a superstitious village. "You're in *love!*" he cries.

I feel my chest clench tight.

My breathing comes a little shallow.

Still grinning, I look away from him, turn my attention back to the tea I'm supposed to be preparing. But AA's too quick.

Before I know it, he's up at my side, hand on my shoulder, leaning that beer-stinking face of his into mine.

"Oh, you've got to tell me all about it," he says, releasing me then taking a couple of steps back.

I tend to the tea, scooping one of the bags up and out of the mulchy-brown liquid, allowing the bag to drip a little of its moisture down into the cup, before lugging it over to the kitchen sink and dumping it there, to be seen to later on.

Perhaps *tomorrow*.

When I've poured a little milk into cups, given each one a stir, I nod in the direction of the kitchen table. "Have you read the diary yet?" I say.

AA's eyes loll back in their sockets, and he does that repulsive thing where he shows me only the whites of his eyes. "Me no like reading," he says, his voice a dull, drawling monotone—like a zombie.

I push past him, arrive back at the table with the cups of tea.

I look down at the diary.

I see that he's hardly made it past the first few pages.

I turn back to AA, who's snatched up his cup of tea, and is wincing at the taste. "Got any sugar?" he says.

I take a seat at the table. "Nope, afraid not."

AA sinks down into the seat opposite mine. "What is this? Wartime Britain?"

I set my cup of tea down on the table then slide the diary across to AA. "Look at the entry for the sixteenth of December."

AA eyes me suspiciously, as if there's some sort of witchcraft involved with that date. He lifts the diary up, rests it in the palm of his hand and then flips through to the entry.

I watch on as his eyes beat from side to side, right to left, from where I'm sitting, drinking in all the text there. When he reaches the end, he leans back in his chair a little, giving himself more distance from the page, as if that might help him bring the message clearer. He peers over the book at me then says, brow furrowed, "Brian Mathewson has a daughter?"

I shrug. "Seems like it."

———

"Who's Mitsy?" AA says, having flipped back to the front of the diary.

I stare at AA as he reads the diary, feeling the tea already swilling through my gut, warming me from within. "I was hoping you could help with that."

AA shakes his head, flips through some more of the pages, and then right back to the front page again. To the dedication. "Brian's handwriting, all right," AA says, "no doubt about that." He looks up at me. "Where'd you get this?"

I think about withholding that information, if only to see the reaction from AA—to see him squirm now that the shoe's on the other foot. But I relent. "Amy handed it to me."

"Amy Douglas?" he says, raising an eyebrow.

"Uh huh."

AA turns back to the diary, flips back to the cover, squints at the golden lettering on the front. "You suppose she could be Brian's daughter?"

"That's what I was thinking," I reply.

AA shakes his head again. "But why do you think she's given this diary to you? It doesn't make any sort of sense."

"Guess there's something she wants me to understand."

AA continues to bat through the pages of the diary as I hear my mobile buzzing away on the kitchen counter. I get lucky the first time, AA doesn't so much as glance in the direction of the mobile, so taken is he by the high-level gossip playing out in that diary in his hand.

When it buzzes again, though, and I make no move to answer, he glances up at me with a wry grin and says, "Don't let *me* get in the way of love, will you?"

My buttocks a little numbed from sitting so long on the wooden kitchen chair, I hoik myself up, see that—*indeed*—it is Mark calling.

Only when I glance to the date on my phone, see that it's *Saturday*, do I realise that I'd agreed to go out and see a film with him tonight.

Our *second* date.

An unpleasant knot forms in my stomach.

I turn back to AA.

And he seems to read me just as easily as that diary he holds in his hands.

Without a word, he sets the diary back down on the kitchen table, gets to his feet, and says, "Come on, let's go get you properly dressed."

————

As I sit in the passenger seat of AA's car—a sleek, black estate, with enough room for a small family in the back—I feel the throbbing vibrations of the engine passing up through my seat. Those vibrations serve only to twist the nerves jangling through my veins.

To make them even more difficult to contend with.

Surprisingly, the car smells pleasantly of lavender, and is still quite clean. For some reason I'd imagined that AA's car would be nothing short of an unmitigated tip:

Greased-up fast-food containers.

Emptied bottles of beer.

The odd condom here and there . . .

But it's actually in fairly decent shape.

The explanation for this orderliness soon becomes apparent, though, as AA goes on to tell me that he only bought it last week.

I chew irritatedly on the peppermint gum AA fed me as I stepped into the car. Even though I realise that we're running late —that I managed to fob Mark off with an excuse of something along the lines of being stuck in traffic—I can't help but feel that AA's driving a touch too fast. We're bombing around corners, shooting our way down too-narrow streets lined with cars on either side.

I can't help but wonder what happened to AA's last car.

But AA gets me to the cinema with impeccable timing.

I swoop to give him a thank-you peck on the cheek, and then totter out of the car, attempting to keep myself upright on the stiletto heels which AA *insisted* I wear for tonight's date. As I feel a cool, autumnal breeze blow along the street, I reach my arms about myself for warmth, glad that AA permitted me the flimsy, silk scarf I have coiled about the exposed area of my upper chest. The light-pink overcoat comes down to only about the cusp of my kneecaps: AA wouldn't allow me any tights.

I can't help but feel that everybody is looking at me and —*more precisely*—my bare legs, wondering just how I'm managing to survive this chilly night.

All of a sudden, I feel like those teenage girls who stand in outdoor queues for nightclubs in nothing more substantial than a *dishcloth* to keep out the cold.

As I listen to the engine of AA's car roar away, I step on in through the automatic, folding doors of the shopping centre, and *clip-clop* my way across the still-wet, disinfectant-stinking floor.

When I get to the multiplex cinema, I spot Mark straight away.

It's actually quite difficult *not* to see him.

Even among a crowd.

Or should that be *especially* among a crowd?

Height can be quite an advantage.

Already with an apology on my lips, I stride past the packed, Saturday night eateries: the Chinese, Mexican and BBQ restaurants; at this time it's mostly adults, dressed smartly, and indulging in some sustenance before their night out.

Like our *first* date, Mark's dressed smart.

Tonight, though, he wears his thick, black hair loose, all fluffed-up and voluminous.

He cradles his brown jacket in his arms and stands exposed in only the light purple shirt he wears underneath. The sleeves rolled back. Hem of the shirt tucked into his smart, black jeans. His shoes gleam in the fluorescent light of the shopping centre.

As I draw close to him, I feel my heart beating hard in my mouth.

Somehow, in my hurry to get through the shopping centre, to not arrive completely—*irretrievably*—late, I managed to swallow my gum. And now I can feel it stuck in my throat. The taste of it bitter and impossible to get rid of without a healthy serving of water, or some other beverage, to work it loose.

As I close in on Mark, I catch that now-familiar odour of sawdust, and of cologne, and *already* it feels like I'm coming home.

. . . I guess I really *am* becoming a ditsy spinster in my middle age.

When I lean into him, ready for those thick, full lips to press up against mine, he takes me by the hand. Before he kisses me, though, I hear his deep, soothing voice.

But it's not what I expect at all.

"This way, Anna," he says. "You're being followed."

Chapter Thirteen

U NABLE TO REALLY ABSORB what his statement means, I feel him take hold of me gently, but firmly, and guide me in through the pseudo Roman-pillared archway of the cinema.

Onto the concourse.

Immediately, I find my senses swamped with the warm stink of buttered popcorn, of the tangy sensation of sugary drinks, and—*still*—that disinfectant which seems to cling to this entire shopping centre.

As Mark leads me down a staircase, guiding me with his hand at the base of my spine, I can't help but think to myself, somewhat giddily, that the cleaning ladies at this shopping centre really do put in their overtime.

We leave behind the obnoxious neon signs; the two-minute, action-packed advertising reels showing off the latest block-busters; the people standing in crowds, some of them slurping on drinks, others with their arms full of cardboard popcorn contain-ers, or steaming hotdogs smothered in mustard and ketchup.

Without another word to me, Mark glances back over my shoulder then pushes hard on the metal bar with a fluorescent strip stuck to it.

The strip reads:

EMERGENCY EXIT

From somewhere, an alarm sounds.

A blunt, flat, *insistent* note.

Right away, I feel the cool night air swill in from the outside, bring my skin immediately up into pimples. But I step through the doorway, and out onto the pavement.

Mark brings the door shut behind us with a firm motion.

The alarm within ceases.

I look through the windows, to the staircase within.

Trying to see anybody who might be following.

But there's no one.

I turn to Mark, but he's already leading me away from the cinema, bringing me clip-clopping alongside him like an obedient pony.

We've got about a hundred metres from the cinema when he can't take it anymore.

When he turns to me, a wide smile smeared across his face.

And he breaks out into a laugh.

I stare at him.

My expression stone-cold: deadly.

I wonder whether I should've brought a gun along with me on this date.

There's a first for everything, I suppose.

I don't need an explanation to see what's going on here, though.

Still feeling his fingers clasped about mine, I slip out of his hold.

And, without pausing to say another word to him, I turn my back, and march away, headed for the rumbling main road, hoping that I might just happen to catch AA whizzing by in his car.

I haven't got half a dozen steps away when I hear Mark call after me.

"Anna! Anna! Wait!"

I think about breaking into a run then remind myself that, considering my footwear, it might not be the best of ideas.

I cross my arms over my chest.

Turn to him.

I glare at a spot right between his eyes.

Mark stops a few paces from me, intelligent enough not to come any closer. He still smiles, but there's a slight sadness in his eyes now.

Nothing like a good joke backfiring, I suppose . . .

"I'm sorry, Anna, it's just what you said before, you know, about being a hired killer? I thought that it might be a good . . ." Mark slaps himself on the forehead, shakes his head and then sinks his teeth into his lower lip. Finally, he looks back up at me. "I'm sorry," he says. "It was a stupid idea."

I play with the idea of giving him forgiveness, but decide to string him along for another few moments.

Nothing good ever comes out of giving men what they want.

Not right away.

As Mark stands before me, a fresh breeze blows between us.

I can't help but give a little shudder.

Feel my teeth chatter together.

And I catch another whiff of his sawdust-and-cologne scent.

Watch that black hair of his tussle in the wind.

"Let's not ruin Saturday night, okay?" Mark says, his voice a little whiney now, but—*irritatingly*—he's beginning to win me over. He meets my eyes then cocks his head. Like a faithful dog, I know that there's nothing I can do to deny him whatever he wants. "I wanted this to be romantic, I thought you'd find it funny . . . I'm sorry."

Having counted the requisite trio of 'sorrys' I decide that now's the time to forgive him. To see just where he's going with all this.

"So," I say, keeping my voice as cool as the breeze near enough turning us to ice, "What's the plan? I suppose we're not going to the pictures after all."

Mark brightens, obviously sensing redemption around the corner.

He takes a step towards me.

I don't back away.

He reaches his hand out to me. "Come on," he says, "I'll show you."

I play with the idea of not accepting, of making him suffer just a few minutes longer, but, in the end, that cologne—that *sawdust*—wins the day for him.

I take hold of his hand, and he guides me away from the roadside.

He leads me down a quiet side street.

Not back to the multiplex cinema.

Already, I feel my anger beginning to flare up again.

Right as I'm on the point of telling him that if there's another joke around the corner then I want no part in it, I notice the archway, illuminated with silver-white fairy lights, looped around the opening. I turn to him, a thousand questions on my lips.

He just smiles back at me, rests his hand at the alcove in my lower back.

Guides me inside.

———

There seems to be no getting around it.

I'm *stunned*.

After walking up a spiral staircase for the best part of—what feels like—half an hour, we emerge out on a rooftop garden. Plants bustle up on all sides, thriving with life—some still flowering, despite the late time of year. Immediately, I'm hit with the thick scent of flowers—what kinds, I'm not certain—but the strength of it is almost sufficient to knock me right over backwards.

Thankfully Mark is keeping a good hold on my lower back.

There're tea lights arranged about the rooftop.

A single fold-out table in the middle of the concrete slabs.

A white tablecloth covering the table and a pair of iron chairs.

Each with a pillow.

A patio heater hangs—almost ominously—above it.

I feel a pounding at my temples, as if I've got a migraine coming on, but I know that it's nothing like a migraine. That, right now, I'm just about as far away from having a migraine as is humanly possible.

Beyond the table and chairs, I make out what can only be described as a 'lovers' seat:' a bench with a larger cushion on it. It hangs low and rocks gently in the light breeze. A patio heater sits over that too, keeping it all warmed up.

The lovers' seat faces a makeshift cinema screen—one of those collapsible devices—and a pair of larger speakers lie on the floor at either side.

I turn to Mark, totally and completely speechless for, perhaps, the very first time in my life. He just grins back at me, smile lines forming all about his mouth and up around his eyes.

He *knows* what he's doing here.

Knows just how to entertain a lady.

And *not bad at all* on a carpenter's salary, if that's what he *really* is . . .

A waiter, wearing a tuxedo, with a white towel draped over his arm, offers us a pair of glasses of clear liquid which sit on his silver tray.

I take one of them.

Have a sip.

A lemony, *zesty* taste.

Lemonade, it follows . . .

That really *is* a first, because, no matter how romantic, or how deep a man's convictions are when it comes to turning down alcohol, I know that those instincts are really put to the test when sex is on the line.

Or the *possibility* of sex.

We'll see . . .

We sit down at the table for half an hour or so, we sip at our drinks, the patio heater keeping us warm. I surprise myself at how easily I've managed to forget all about the 'joke' earlier and Mark, too, seems to have allowed it to slip from his mind.

I find myself making allowances for him.

How *was* he to know that I was being serious the other night?

How serious does saying something like that come across?

Soon after, we move to the lovers' seat, before the unfolded screen.

To begin with, I sit over to one side.

I might be *impressed* but that doesn't mean I'm suddenly going to become some Jezebel.

Mark signals to the waiter, and the screen fills with light.

I suppose that the whole routine of sitting at the table before-hand was some sort of a strategy to get me accustomed to being up on the rooftop, because, for the first few minutes that I arrived up here, I found myself distracted by the view—by the buildings shooting up on either side of us, the multiplex several floors below: squat and ugly from this perspective.

I guess the architects never did account for people like us.

Sitting up here.

On the roof.

As the film taps through its story—a black-and-white, *romantic* affair, which I soon forget anything at all about—I slide on up beside Mark.

Feel his body heat against my thigh.

Before I *really* know what I'm doing, I reach out and around him, pass my arm over his shoulder. Almost as if *I'm* the guy, and *he's* the girl, I draw him towards me.

We kiss.

As the old-style, American-accented voices jabber on about this, that, or the other, I reach my hand down to the zipper of his trousers. Feel that, already, he's quite taken by the situation.

After a quick glance-around, I see that the waiter isn't here any longer.

That he's—*wisely*—left us in peace.

And so we begin the main feature.

Chapter Fourteen

I FEEL THE IMPULSE to reach out and jab AA's chin upwards, to stop his jaw from latching open. Right at the moment, I have a Grade-A view into AA's mouth . . . can see all the black fillings which mottle his molars.

With a shake of his head, AA dips his eyes down to his over-priced coffee, takes a sip of the white froth then wipes the foam off his lips with the back of his hand. "You *slut!*" he says.

I glance around me.

Once more, I absorb the hot air of Café Rouge.

The windows are all steamed up, and I can tell from the dull, grey shine on the inside of the panes that it's grim outside. No doubt there's still drizzle falling. Traffic tailed back all the way around the corner. Dour faces peering out over steering wheels, hoping to get home.

In the café, I glance about the people packed into seats, and the several more hovering about the counter, clutching their ordered coffees; surreptitiously trying to eye an empty table, the more forward among them glaring at the students absorbed by their laptops, their coffees long ago emptied; the free wifi very much still flowing.

Behind the counter, one of the baristas gives the milk churner a couple of goes.

I feel the warm, milky steam carry through the air. Feel it settle against my skin. It smells almost sour, and it's a touch bitter on my tongue.

I recline against the hard back of my polished-up wooden chair, gaze over the table at AA, watching him shake his head at me.

He peers down into his coffee, swipes it up, and then downs it in one.

Just like he treats *all* his beverages.

Hot *and* cold.

He brings his now-empty coffee cup back down with a decisive, porcelain *chink* on its saucer, sending the spoon tinkling. I notice several of those waiting by the counter for a seat shifting hopeful glances in our direction.

Yeah, well, they can hope away, because I've still very much got a cup of coffee in front of me. And I have no intention of 'downing it' like AA . . . I *savour* my drinks . . .

I peel back the sleeves of my jumper to the elbow. I smooth the sweat from my palms on the thigh of my jeans, and give AA the slickest, *smuggest* smile imaginable. "At least *one* of us is getting some."

AA again shakes his head, opens his mouth wide as if I've just mortally offended him.

But we both know that it's the truth.

Despite AA's newly ostentatious lifestyle, he's not exactly beating the boys off with a paddle. I think about what happened a couple of weeks back, at my house.

While we were having tea, I spotted a sash of grey in the side of his hair. After I mentioned it, I thought that the only way to get him *out* of my house would be with the help of a specialist *team*, judging by the amount of time he spent staring at himself in the mirror out in the hall, dejectedly attempting to hide said spot with a quick comb-over job.

It had little effect.

AA reels himself back in, and I examine his black leather jacket, which he wears over a black t-shirt, with the neck stretched out. He certainly has all the hallmarks of being a Mid-Life Crisis Case, and yet, at the same time, I can't help but think that the *whole* of AA's life has just been one *long* mid-life crisis.

"So," AA says, apparently admitting that I've got him beaten for now, "I'm sure you'd like to know the reason *why* I asked you here today, to this fine establishment."

I glance about Café Rouge, and resist the temptation to tell him that there's one of these on just about every street corner of the UK. And then to ask him just *who* he takes me for . . . but I allow him his little joke—he's *hurting*, after all.

The truth is that the common trait I observe in all these Café Rouges is that there's crumbs, screwed-up, used napkins, and a general sense of disorder within.

As I make to rest my arms on the table in front of me, I notice a crumb, flick it out of the way, onto the floor, and then say, to AA, "Go on. Enlighten me."

AA dips his hand into the inside pocket of his leather jacket.

From within, he produces the diary.

My eyeballs almost roll out of their sockets. "I didn't give you that!"

AA shoots me a smirk back. He slaps the diary down on the

table between us. He purses his lips as if he's the one who should be on the receiving end of an apology. "Since you didn't go to the liberty of making me a copy, I had to take extreme measures."

"You broke in again?" I say.

"Hardly," AA says, closing one eye and giving the campest of hand waves—something which he *never* does, and which he only does now to mock me. "Your neighbour, Mrs Pietersen, she's *certainly* a dear. Gave me the spare key when I told her I was your *boyfriend*."

I feel my throat close up a little.

And, truth be told, taste some sick at the back of my mouth.

Obviously AA didn't need *anybody* else to get into my house— he could've let himself in just like the hundreds of times he's done before . . . but *no*, he has to make it a *challenge*.

I *knew* it was a mistake to give Mrs Pietersen a spare key, and I think long and hard about how I might go about persuading my octogenarian neighbour to hand it back over.

Without breaking her heart, of course, if at all possible . . .

"Look," AA continues, "this is neither here nor there—do you want to hear what I've got, or what?"

"Yes," I say, my tone impatient, which is just as well, because my *mood's* impatient too.

AA leans in over the table. His voice drops to a whisper, as if someone with *any* sort of interest in this might be present in the café with us. "I think what Amy Douglas was trying to tell you— what she wanted to let you know by giving you *this* diary"—he gives it a slap—"is . . ." he trails off.

If we weren't in a crowded location, and I could be sure that I could get away with it without some *well-meaning* bystander getting involved, I'd club him right over his left eye.

But I don't.

I hold still.

"What?" I say. "Is this Saturday-night TV, or something?"

AA smiles to himself, looks down at the diary before him. "Amy wanted to show you that *she* knows *just* who she is . . ."

"Uh huh," I say, resting my head on my hand, then, remembering my coffee, and hoping it'll give me a kick to get through this conversation, I take a sip.

AA smiles wider still.

I realise that *this* is the punch coming.

"She also wanted to tell you that Brian has no idea who *she* is."

I feel myself sink a little into the chair, and yet my surroundings stay quite still. I'm aware of the chatter in the café growing quiet. I feel cold all of a sudden.

And then I realise.

It comes to me as one of those *annoying* playground rhymes.

I know something Brian doesn't know . . .

———

Although I try my best to get a ride off AA back home, he turns me down, feeds me that old line of 'going in the opposite direction.' I suppose that I can't *really* blame him, given the rush-hour traffic and all . . . still, he's not the one who has to squeeze in under somebody's armpit on the Tube to get home.

It starts raining seemingly the second I set foot on the pavement outside the station, and I haven't brought an umbrella along with me . . . no, that would've required *foresight.*

So, sopping wet, and feeling like I've got something gravitationally challenged sitting on my chest, I approach my garden gate which, as always, could do with a lick of paint . . . or a merciful scrap merchant. I notice the huddled-up bundle of blankets in my front garden.

Leaning up against the wall, apparently asleep.

I take a step towards said bundle of blue-grey blankets, expecting that cacophony of odours: the mixture of sewage, and liquor, and whatever else this homeless person has rolled in.

Strangely, though, I get none of those scents at all.

The rain patters down into the plastic guttering above my head, and feeling a fresh chill move through me, I cross my arms over my chest. Even though it feels like my throat might well have swallowed itself, I manage to get out, "Hey, you can't sleep here." I pause for a second, then add, "Private property."

The bundle shifts a little—its tiny world disrupted.

All shook up.

Then, from within the blankets, I see a pink face emerge.

Blond hair framing the face.

Sapphire eyes latch onto mine.

"Anna?"

Chapter Fifteen

I GET AMY into the house, and, without saying anything at all, I hand her a towel and point her up the stairs. As I listen to her trudge her way up the staircase, sending the long-suffering floorboards creaking out in protest, I stick the kettle on, sit down at the table and wonder how the hell my life came to this.

In truth, I never wanted to be a mother.

That was all my ex-husband—*Arnold's*—idea.

Being an only child, I've not really had much experience being a *sister* either.

Let alone a *Big Sister*.

I dig out a chocolate biscuit and chew on it as I listen to the random *pitter-patter* of the rain against the windows compete with the mechanical *whine* of the electric heating unit upstairs in the shower.

It's a hell of a night to sleep rough.

To be *thinking* about sleeping rough.

Lizzie seems to agree, and she arrives up at my calves, as

always rubbing her chubby, furry body against me, almost seeming to pulse warmth directly into my bloodstream.

I pick her up and set her on my lap, feeling something like a Bond villain as I stroke her head, staring at the kitchen doorway, waiting for Amy to descend, and explain herself.

When I do hear her, clicking off the shower, pausing just a moment to discover the *dry* clothes of mine I've left outside the bathroom for her; I feel a damp lump down the side of my leg. With a *yowl* of protest, I scoop Lizzie off my lap, and slip my hand into my pocket.

From within, I discover the diary.

Sopping wet.

Of course it is.

I look to the pages, see how the black ink has become mottled into the paper.

When I try to peel the diary open, several of the pages tear.

I hope that this diary didn't hold any sort of a special place in Amy's heart.

Then again, considering that she *gave* it to me—knowing that I'm hardly the most responsible person in the world—she might think a little harder about who she trusts in future.

Just a tip.

I'm attending to the teapot when Amy comes wandering in.

I find it somewhat appalling that, despite the fact the silver tracksuit bottoms and V-necked sports shirt I loaned her are clearly a size—or *three*—too large for her, she still looks absolutely stunning. But maybe it's because she's just stepped out of the shower.

That's got to be it.

That baby-pink glow to her cheeks.

My eyes drift down to her neck, to the spot where the dog bit her.

I can see a little scarring, and can tell that there's a spot of plastic surgery afoot, but, aside from that, the mark is hardly noticeable.

With a waft from my lime-scented shower gel, she circles one of the kitchen chairs, hovers a second and then sits.

Good girl.

She meets my eye, attempts a half smile, fails, and then goes back to staring into space.

I pour a couple of cups of tea, ask her if she takes milk and sugar, and she answers in the affirmative each time. I don't think to press her for details like quantities, it seems like she's had such a rough day that she just doesn't have the resistance for that.

Without saying anything else, I hand her a cup of tea.

She wraps her fingers about it.

Only then do I realise that I've left the sodden diary in the middle of the table.

Amy looks long and hard at the diary, then turns her attention back, downwards, into her cup of tea.

I lean up against the kitchen counter, take my cup of tea in my hands, and feel the warming waves passing through my skin. "Want to tell me how you got hold of my address?"

Another smile traces Amy's lips.

But it disappears just as quickly.

She looks at me, then says, "I'm Brian Mathewson's daughter, remember?" She looks away, and, I think, just for a second, that there're a few glistening tears in her eyes. "You can find anybody if you really want to."

It's funny, looking at Amy now, in profile, I can sort of see the outline of Brian's features. That stubby nose. The *overfilled* lips. A slight redness to her complexion which, in retrospect, might offer Brian something of a riposte to what I've always considered an 'alcoholic' glow to his face.

It was genetics all along.

———

I wait till Amy has finished her tea before befuddling her with questions.

But when I do ask them, I don't hold back.

I demand to know, first of all, what she's doing here, at my house.

She feeds me that old cliché about 'not having anywhere else to go.'

Yeah, right, a bright, affable girl like herself.

The Chief Constable's daughter.

Not likely.

Back when she was a police officer she did her very best to hide her roots, to not allow anyone to think that she was a supreme sample of nepotistic success. She even went as far as to run that whole routine of switching out her father's surname—Branwick—for her mother's—Douglas. It seems that she *always* counted on Daddy's protection.

Can't she count on it now?

I collect up her emptied mug of tea, dump it into the sink with a metallic *clatter* which spooks Lizzie, sends her streaming out around the doorway to the kitchen. I give each mug a quick squirt of washing-up liquid—the stuff that smells, *oddly*, of mint —and then give each a quick blast from the hot-water tap; scalding my hands as I do so.

When I return to the table, sucking on one of my affected

fingers, tasting that rubbery flavour of my own skin, I see that Amy is back to her standard pose:

Staring into space.

I settle back in the chair opposite her. Clutch my hands together and rest my wrists on the wooden surface, almost imagining myself as a police officer, interviewing a witness in a windowless room around the back of the station. "So why did your father allow you to get into this whole assassination game at all?"

Amy stays quiet for a long few moments, and I wonder if she might've slipped off to some other dimension. If she's done what psychiatrists like to term 'escape.'

But she does answer my question.

Her tone a little shaky.

Her voice lacking any sort of power.

"You need to understand something," she says, "about my father—and about *Brian*."

I note how, despite the obvious truth, she still refers to Chief Constable Charlie Branwick as her 'father' and Brian by his first name.

"The two of them have been friends for so long," she continues, "back when they were both much younger, back when my father was a simple *plod*"—here there's a slight wince in her voice, as if she imagines her father might be standing in the doorway, listening into her speaking about him in disrespectful tones—"he and Brian would meet up on Friday nights, at a shitty little bar called *Oakland*."

" '*Oakland?*' " I say, as if I'm actually a police officer, butting in to confirm a specific detail.

"Uh huh," she says, "back then Brian wasn't much himself, either, just a local reporter. But they became friends." A sly smile twists her lips. "They used to call themselves the Cold Case Club."

"And why was that?"

She meets my eye for a fraction of a second, but it's long enough for her to roll her eyes and shake her head. "*Think* about it."

I do . . .

Beer: cold.

Case of beer.

Cold Case Club.

I give myself a mental box around the ears for ignorance, then turn my attention back to Amy. As she speaks, she doesn't meet my eye, it's as if she's transfixed by the patterned design of my kitchen table.

"They'd chat about cases," she says, "they'd dig up these old, unsolvable mysteries, and try to solve them for themselves."

"Sort of like vigilantes?" I put in.

Amy snorts, gives a shake of her head. "Yeah, except vigilantes actually *do* something—as far as I know, all that Brian and my father got up to was enlarging their stomachs, and escaping their wives."

"This was before you were born?"

Amy looks me in the eye.

There's a sparkle there.

"I was just getting to that part," she says.

———

While I go about brewing another pot of tea, and Lizzie yowls at me to get doing something about her dinner, Amy explains the situation.

Tells me how Brian and her father got close.

How Brian was married to his wife—Michelle: 'Mitsy.'

And about how, after one long night of fighting, Mitsy—Amy's mother—left Brian and showed up on the doorstep of the only place she felt she could go.

Something about *this* part of the tale is beginning to feel a little too familiar for comfort.

Amy explains how Mitsy, her mother, knew that Charlie Branwick secretly fawned after her. Knew how he would treat her like a goddess . . . treat her the way that Brian had never been able to.

"Oh," Amy continues, "I have no doubts that Brian was the love of her life"—she glances down at the sodden diary—"but she thought that she could make a better life for herself with Charlie, with my father; a better life for her baby."

I feel an unpleasant twisting feeling down in my stomach. I pour out another couple of cups of tea, a splash of milk into each, and a dollop of sugar too . . . it feels like we need it.

I sit back down at the table.

"Where's your mother now?" I ask.

Amy gives a nonchalant shrug, coupled with a pout.

She won't meet my eye.

I feel the heat oozing off my cup of tea, and I savour the sensation.

But I still feel that unpleasant twisting sensation down in my gut.

"Amy?" I say. "I'd like to hear the truth."

All of a sudden, Amy turns on me, her eyes wide, nostrils flared. Those blue eyes that were once so delicate—so *beautiful*—are sharp, and deadly. "She died, Anna," she gets out, as if it was bile, "a year ago now." She pauses for a moment as if she's having trouble forming her lips around the word. When she finally does pronounce the word, it's with a deep-lying grudge. "*Cancer*," she adds, and then drops her head down into her folded arms on the kitchen table.

––––––––

There're times when you can just feel the tension *crackling* through the air, and this moment, in my kitchen, is one of those.

I feel my chest drawing tight, and when I attempt to take a sip of tea, I almost choke on it.

Unable to swallow.

I know all about families.

All about *suffering*.

Both my parents are dead and buried.

Neither one went quietly.

Not in the end.

As Amy lies stretched out there, her head stuffed into her arms on my kitchen table, I can't help but feel the tenderness within. As if somebody, up in the middle of the night, has replaced my core of steel with nothing more substantial than marshmallows.

I reach out and, gently, stroke my fingertips across the back of Amy's hand.

Although I expect to find her skin soft, I feel that it's a little rugged, that Amy's not been adhering to her moisturising regime.

"Amy?" I say. "Amy?"

But she won't respond.

I can feel each *sniffle* wrack her body like rapid gunfire.

Something catches my eye, over Amy's head.

In the doorway of the kitchen.

I take a moment to realise that it's my cat, Lizzie.

I watch Lizzie's delicate cat face sniff at the air. She twitches her tail, as if judging the quality of the air in the room. Then she turns her attention to the table. Her slender, oval pupils fix onto Amy—onto Amy's back.

Without pause, Lizzie slips her way across the kitchen floor, and up to Amy's leg. She brushes herself against Amy, gives a sympathetic *miaow-purr*.

Amy stays in the same position for a couple of moments, then she straightens up, looks around. Then down. Notices Lizzie there, at her feet. With a slight smile among the tear tracks which trawl down her cheeks, she puts her arms around Lizzie's willing body.

Brings her up onto her lap.

Loses her fingers in her fur.

I see the smile on Amy's face grow a little stronger.

Pin back her cheeks.

The smile almost seems to begin to dry those tears.

For a long few moments, the two of us are transfixed by the cat between us, as if Lizzie knows how to make herself centre stage. Then, with another *sniff*, Amy looks beyond Lizzie, and to me. She says, "My mother left me the diary—in her will—she never once showed it to Charlie, never told him who I *really* was . . . that Charlie wasn't my real father."

Here she threatens to break down again, but Lizzie, apparently sensing the impending storm, rubs her cat head up against Amy's forearm—*reassuring her*.

"Tonight," Amy continues, then shakes her head vigorously as if she believes that she's trapped in some sort of a dream—a *nightmare*, "I decided that I had to tell him, that I couldn't live with the secret." She stares long and hard into my eyes, her teeth sunken into her lower lip. "I thought that he would understand, that *my father* would understand something like that." She shakes her head again, but this time it's more controlled. "But he didn't understand—not at all. He ordered me out of the house, *away* from him. Never to come back."

My heart sinks in my chest.

I turn my attention back to Lizzie, in Amy's arms.

And I think, *It must all be so much simpler, in a cat's world . . .*

Chapter Sixteen

O F COURSE I allow Amy to stay.

  I tell her that she can stay for as long as she wants, and although people are saying that all the time, I really do mean it.

When I attempt to get to the bottom of Amy's current status, it seems to be somewhere between 'runaway' and 'fugitive.'

She absolutely *doesn't* feel safe leaving the house.

Is clearly worried that her adoptive father will bring the law to bear on her.

I ask her whether I should expect a dawn raid and she assures me that 'it shouldn't come to that.'

When I try to draw from her just what's been going on between Brian and Charlie Branwick, she doesn't seem to know any real details. And I can't help but get that sinking feeling that she's being used as a pawn in some game that she has no hope of understanding.

Brian, like everything else, has *very* complicated relationships with his friends.

And even *more* complicated relationships with his enemies.

. . . Let's not get started on *children* . . .

Speaking of work—of *Brian*—everything remains quiet for a couple of weeks.

And it's not like I'm going to ring him up to solicit *something*.

Truth be told, I'm more than occupied looking after Amy—doing my best to watch for all those 'warning signs' that people in intensely stressful situations are supposed to show.

To be quite honest, I actually find myself quite enjoying the situation.

I've always thought of myself as the stereotypical *loner*, but living with a girl—living with *Amy*—begins to show me that, perhaps, I'm not a lost cause after all.

For those weeks, I hardly leave the house, spending all my time tending to Amy.

We watch films together:

Chick flicks.

Critique the factual blunders in action films.

Get through entire series of TV shows.

Then there're the board games.

And one fateful afternoon sees Amy digging through my wardrobe, giving it the injection of youth it 'so badly needs' . . . apparently.

To be quite honest, I forget about my life—if that's what you could call it—and it's not until I get a phone call from Mark one evening that I remember all about our fledgling romance.

He tells me something slightly baffling, about how my son, Ben, and his son, Nathan, are going on a football-training weekend.

It involves camping.

Outdoors stuff.

When I ask Mark just what exactly the kids get out of it, he says 'team bonding' in a way which sounds, to me, that he's just as baffled by the idea as I am.

But I agree to it.

Just one weekend.

As with all the plans involving my kids, I get in touch with Arnold, arrange it with him. He sounds glad that I've decided to pick up the ball on this one, albeit a touch surprised. And I can only put it down to *surprise* which leads him to ask if I'd take my daughter—Ben's younger sister—Josie along with us too.

Not seeing any reason why I *shouldn't* accept, I do.

When I set my mobile phone back down on the kitchen counter, I imagine to myself about how Arnold and Kate, right at this moment, are exchanging a flying high-five.

A dirty weekend for them.

When I turn around, I see that Amy is standing in the doorway to the kitchen. I notice that she's wearing a pair of short shorts which she instructed me to 'throw out.'

She's lugging Lizzie in her arms, cuddling her up to her chest.

The two of them have got quite thick since Amy moved in.

When I meet Amy's eye, she gives me a faint smile then turns away.

Heads into the sitting room.

I listen to the TV gargle into life.

Guess I forgot *one* facet of childcare.

———

On Friday evening, and all set for my unexpected camping trip, I look over my hard-shell suitcase and the pair of squashy, daypacks sitting in the hallway, unable to clear my mind of the idea that I *surely* don't have everything I need here.

Not to get through a *whole* weekend out in the wilderness.

I tell myself what I've *already* told myself about a thousand times.

If you want to take it, Anna, you'll have to carry it.

And I have little intention of doing *too much* carrying.

Since my kids are coming along for this weekend, I need to stay as hands free as possible, ready for any sort of emergency that might arise.

As I hear the *rumble* of the car engine idling outside, I check myself over in the mirror. Although it was with the aid of my professional fashion consultant—*Amy*—that I picked out my outfits, I can't help but think, looking myself over, seeing the black zip-up fleece over the all-weather black trousers, that I seem ready to go to work.

Like I'm going to be getting some killing done on the camping trip.

Smart, business-like footsteps sound along the garden path outside, and, before they get the chance to ring the bell, I open up the front door.

I take in AA standing there.

He looks *dapper* . . . no other word for it:

A smart, pinstriped jacket over the top.

Clean, pink shirt peeping out through the gap.

And tucked into a pair of pinstriped dress trousers.

He stands there with a hand dangling from his pocket.

"Alderknot Babysitting Services," he says, with a shit-eating grin.

I couldn't think of anybody else to call for this *delicate* situation, so I called up AA. Even now, I can't help thinking to myself that, perhaps, Mrs Pietersen next door might've been a better choice, even if her background in household security is a little patchy.

"Amy's through there," I say, pointing in the direction of the sitting room.

In the hallway, still fiddling with the seemingly *thousands* of straps and plastic buckles, I listen to the introductions in the sitting room.

For some reason, I thought AA and Amy had already met—that they knew one another somehow . . . but, I suppose, from the way that they ask one another what their *names* are, that they don't.

Finished with my twiddling for the time being, I shuttle into the sitting room, look AA and Amy over. I can't help noticing, from the way that AA's hanging back, not having taken a seat in one of the armchairs to watch TV with Amy; and from the way that Amy sits slouched to one side of the sofa, eyeballing the screen; that this isn't the warmest of unions.

As if glad that I've come to the rescue, to break the ice, the two of them turn to me with smiles on their faces. I look to Amy. "AA will take good care of you," I say, "if you need anything, you've got my number."

When I look back to Amy, I see that there's a slight smile clinging to her mouth. "Anna?" she says, "Can I have a word out in the hall?"

A little taken aback by the request, but seeing no reason to deny it, I leave AA standing there, in the sitting room, looking a dozen shades of awkward.

I bring the door to the sitting room shut, and turn to Amy.

"Look," I say, "it's just for a weekend—nothing more—I'll be back on Sunday evening . . . just two nights."

Amy's smile widens. She gives me a disbelieving shake of the head. "Anna," she says, her voice dipping down in volume, "did you really think that I was getting desperate? That if you didn't do something, I'd go snooping through your knickers drawer looking for some playtime?"

I hope, by that comment, she hasn't discovered my battery-powered companion.

Probably not.

I feel my chest loosening a little as realisation dawns on me.

I could *really* have some fun here.

But outside I hear another car rolling up, and know, on instinct, that it's Mark.

And I really need the few seconds before he rings my bell to anally go over all of my bags again, to see if any aspect of my appearance has come unstuck in the past ten minutes.

"AA's not that sort of guy," I say.

Amy smiles wider. "Oh, you brought me a *gentleman!*"

I look myself over in the mirror a final time, lug my pair of day bags up—one over either shoulder—prop my hard-shell suit-case up onto its wheels.

Amy doesn't offer to help me with any of the carrying.

But, then again, I suppose it's somewhat understandable considering that she's caught in a sort of man-fever.

As I slip out of the door, I feel that I *should* say something a little more concrete. So, as Amy shuts the door behind me, I tell her.

"The thing with AA," I say, "he's got an intolerance for the fairer sex."

The look of pure confusion on Amy's face remains stamped on my mind's eye.

It tickles me as I stride along the path, towards Mark's waiting estate car.

Brings me out in a wide, wide smile.

Chapter Seventeen

TICK-TICK-TICK.

I give the gas canister my fiercest of glares.

But it doesn't do any good.

What I've discovered, only hours following my submergence into nature, is that nature doesn't take kindly to impatience.

Much less *anger.*

I squeeze the plastic igniting stick a little tighter.

My finger hovers over the button.

Ready to send up another spark.

Maybe the bastard gas will light *this time*.

All around me, I can hear birdsong. I can smell the earth, coupled with that damp scent of leaves—it was raining when we arrived here. I try not to think about the tins of baked beans we have to heat up for tonight's dinner. I fail, already fantasising about the rich, tomato sauce, the grainy texture of the beans. The thought makes my stomach gurgle.

I look back to the *unlit* gas stove.

The useless plastic lighting stick I hold in my hand.

At this rate, we'll be lucky to be eating at midnight.

Whenever I turn around, look back over my shoulder to the campsite: a regulation hundred metres away from the camp*fire* spot; I see Mark, his son Nathan; my two kids: Josie and Ben; all laughing away at Mark's, no doubt hilarious, joke.

They are all sprawled about in camp chairs; the tents already erected behind them.

A little further behind, Mark's car sits dark, and looming, almost as if it's jealous of the fun that's being had.

Further away still, are the other tents.

All the other parents accompanying their children for this 'team-building' weekend.

Everybody seems to be having a good time.

Everybody *except* me.

Right as I turn back to the gas stove, determined that *this*— out of the other thousand, or so, attempts I've already made— will be the time, I notice a whole group of kids with wide smiles chewing on steaming-hot hamburgers some smug parent has prepared them.

When the gas stove doesn't light this time, I toss the plastic lighting stick off into the undergrowth where it will remain, forever more, lost to civilisation.

———

I lie on my back in my tent, staring at the canvas roof.

The rain patters down.

I can smell its salty scent on the air.

Penetrating the fabric of the tent even.

In the tent alongside, I can hear Josie and Ben chatting away in low tones—not quite having got over the novelty of sharing the same sleeping space.

Something which they probably believed they'd got shot of once their ages had reached double figures. Guess they hadn't bargained for *camping*.

Despite the cool, October air outside, I feel somewhat *cosy* in my sleeping bag, all tucked up. I have to admit that I half considered investing in a portable electric heater specifically for this camping trip . . . when I referred the matter to Amy, she assured me that I wasn't totally out of my mind in considering it.

But, in the end, I decided to suck it up; take this experience on the chin.

I hear Mark's footsteps outside before I hear his gruff voice.

Much closer than I would've imagined.

Almost as if he was speaking right into my ear.

"Anna?" he says, in a whisper. "Are you asleep?"

"Yes," I say, rolling my eyes and shaking my head at the stupidity of the question.

"Ah, all right," he says, "in that case I should come back in the morning."

I wait for him to leave, but hear none of his retreating footfalls.

Instead, I hear the slight *ripping* sound of the zip being dragged down and, before I know it, Mark's on his hands and knees in the darkness of the tent.

I continue to lie on my back, eyeballing him as if he was some sort of spirit.

With the voices of Josie and Ben still jabbering on about—whatever it is that a thirteen-year-old and a ten-year-old jabber on about—Mark arrives beside me.

He lies on his side.

I can just see his outline from the weak light which ekes in through the opening in the tent which Mark failed to zip shut behind him. He's wearing just what he was earlier on: khaki shirt, loose trousers, and a pair of sturdy walking boots which he promptly kicks off into the porch area of the tent.

"How's camping treating you so far?" he says.

I turn to him with a slight smile. "I think we understand one another's *differences*."

"Those beans were out of this world," he says.

Although I have the urge to give him one of those numbing punches on his upper arm, I restrain myself, tell myself that countryside violence never got anyone anywhere.

Stifling a yawn, I say, "I guess the people working the conveyor belt, where they tin up the beans, really pulled a blinder that shift."

I feel him draw closer to me.

I breathe in his slight scent of sawdust.

Feel one of his rugged—*'honest'*—hands brush my cheek.

"I really like you, Anna," he says. "And our kids seem to be getting along fine."

Right now, I imagine that Nathan is lying back in Mark's tent, snoring away; while my two kids refuse to go to sleep for the time being . . . too much excitement, and all that.

I cast my mind back to earlier on in the day, and I have to admit that Mark's right.

Our kids *did* seem to get along fine.

Although Mark warned me that Nathan and Ben don't hang around much at school, they could've fooled me by the way they were laughing and joking with one another.

"Would you like to get a little cosy?" Mark says, and his voice *really does* sound that seedy.

"The zipper's on your side," I say, referring to the sleeping bag.

Mark fumbles about in the darkness, apparently having some difficulty.

That's a change.

Finally, he does manage to pull the zipper free, or—to put it more bluntly—he *yanks* it downwards making a not-very-subtle *ziiip!*

I feel his thick, well-muscled legs up against mine.

His powerful arms circling my shoulders.

He shifts himself a little closer to me and then lets out a muffled cry.

"What?" I say. "What is it?"

Mark reaches beneath him, retrieves a blocky object. "It's your phone." He hands it over to me, and I rest it down beside my pillow.

It's when Ben and Josie have gone quiet in the tent alongside, and when Mark is silently kissing my neck that I feel a chilly dawning of realisation.

I wriggle out from underneath Mark, wrap my paw about my phone.

"What?" Mark says. "What is it?"

I tap the screen into life.

Yep, sure enough, there it is.

Low battery.

Chapter Eighteen

I SPEND A GOOD DEAL of the next morning asking around the campsite for a phone charger, but, for some inexplicable reason, nobody has one which'll fit the make of my phone. I go through my luggage three—*or four?*—times searching for the charger but can't find it anywhere . . . if only I'd brought it, I could've plugged it into one of the many power stations located about the campsite.

But, as things stand, I'll be cut off until I return home on Sunday night.

Noticing my slightly ruffled state, Mark squeezes my shoulder and mumbles in my ear, "Worried about missing a lucrative job?"

A nervous tingle passes through my blood, followed swiftly by rising anger.

But I manage to block out those feelings.

To tell myself that Mark's just 'playing around' . . . that he really has no idea.

No idea *at all*.

I manage to press on a smile.

Mark takes a step away from me. "If it's really important, you can get in touch using my phone, or Nathan's—it'd just be a case of switching out the cards, both of our phones are unlocked."

I steady myself, calm myself down.

I glance about the campsite, see the parents shuffling back and forth with their offspring.

Every last one of them beaming.

I reassure myself that Amy's in good hands.

She has AA there, and, if it comes to it, she has Lizzie . . . although, admittedly, Lizzie's not really much in terms of an attack cat; perhaps, one of these days, I should get around to training her . . .

And, I have to admit, the prospect of me passing anything to do with my phone into another person's possession—no matter how *short* a time—really doesn't appeal to me.

And least of all to a child.

I placate Mark with a ditsy smile, and a catty, "If it's so important then they can let me know on Monday morning."

Mark smiles back at me, gives a nod.

What I wouldn't give to be as *clueless* as him.

While Ben and Nathan go off with their football coach for some 'circuit drills'—something which sounds *suspiciously* Army-like—me and Mark take a walk with Josie in tow. As we go along the beaten-in bridle path which runs around the back of the campsite, we surreptitiously hold hands as Josie skips about ahead of us, apparently riding an invisible horsey or something.

Ploughed fields stretch away from us on either side, and I can smell the gentle scent of manure on the breeze . . . it brings back memories of that disastrous hit I shared with Amy.

That bite on her throat.

As I feel Mark's calloused hands squeeze mine, I can't help thinking to myself—*wondering*—whether Amy believes if anything was afoot . . . if it was just a case of slouchy timing, or if I actively decided to pause, to allow the dog to *bite* her . . .

Even if she does have such an inkling then surely—*hopefully*—all will now be forgiven.

After the weeks we've spent together.

Getting to *know* one another.

I listen to the wind rustle the leaves in the trees alongside the bridle path, and I keep an eye—dare I say a *motherly eye?*—on Josie as she trots back into view.

It's then, everything peaceful, *placid*, that Mark turns to me and says, "You know, Anna, I'd like to learn more about you." He looks me in the eye with those hazel irises of his. Then he looks away, back along the path. "It feels as if you know all about me."

Although this is *patently* untrue, I decide not to fight it.

I know that it'll leave me at a distinct disadvantage.

Because I *do* have something to hide.

"What'd you like to know?" I say, already scolding myself for giving him such a wide gateway to my private world.

"Oh, I dunno," he replies, "just something—your *hobbies?*"

"My hobbies?"

I really haven't had time to register the question when I hear Josie calling out to us, telling us to hurry up otherwise she's going to leave us behind.

With a mutual smile, we break off our hand holding and jog to catch her up.

———

That evening, our last evening of camping—*thank God*—we sit around an actual, real-life campfire that I might, or might not, have had a hand in creating. We tell scary stories.

And, just like all the best campfire-storytelling sessions, we each sit on a log.

I sit beside Josie, feel her clinging to my side, and wonder if —for a ten-year-old girl—this really might be the best of activities.

Ben and Nathan sit on another log; Ben subconsciously whittling a stick into a sharp point with his pen knife, while Nathan sits crossed-legged and bounces his foot.

We're all listening to Mark.

I sit opposite Mark, staring through the flames at him.

As he tells us the story—about a girl, and ghost, which I hardly follow—he never takes his eyes off me.

I comb my fingers through Josie's soft hair, and feel her drifting off quietly, leaning up against my side. I'm aware of the rest of the campsite—the other parents and their offspring—all sitting around their own fires, and playing out their own version of the last night of camping.

Mark wraps up the story, telling us that the little girl, who'd followed the ghost—for reasons only known to herself—tumbled down into a tomb she had uncovered in her back garden. And, when she hit the bottom of the earthy pit, she heard the stone lid grind into place over her head.

Nobody came to answer her screams.

I glance over to the two boys: to Nathan and Ben, announce that it's time for everybody to go to bed. In response to this command, I feel Josie's fingers burrow into my flesh and take hold . . . not doing wonders for my self-esteem—I suppose that sitting about the house for a few weeks is the perfect route to weight gain; maybe I should write a book . . .

All three kids, albeit reluctantly, hoik themselves up and off to their respective tents.

I find myself alone with Mark, who, acknowledging that we really *are* alone, rounds the embers of the campfire and takes up his place on the log beside me.

I can feel that my buttocks have gone a touch numb from sitting about on the hard surface of the log for so long, but I do my best to keep *that* thought within my head.

There's a myriad of details that fledgling lovers really don't need to know.

"So," Mark says, his voice low—*sexy*, "you never did get round to answering my question earlier this afternoon."

"No," I say, only now remembering.

"Tell me something about yourself, Anna."

I hold still, and can't hide the fact that I've stiffened up every muscle in my body. I feel as if I'm resisting Mark's touch, as if I'm trying to hold him at an arm's length . . . and, I suppose, in reality, I *am*.

I swallow hard, feeling my throat dry . . . much drier than I'd thought.

I suppose that's an occupational hazard of sitting by a campfire for hours on end.

"Well," I begin, "actually, these past few weeks, I've taken in a colleague."

Mark holds me tight. He smiles at me.

Obviously willing me to continue.

"She's not been doing so well—trouble in her personal life—so I asked her if she'd like to come and stay with me for a while."

"What's her name?" Mark says, his delicious eyes tracing mine.

I hesitate, wondering what the best way forward here is.

Then decide that it can't hurt.

"Amy," I reply.

"Amy," he answers, as if confirming my words, to be used against me at a later date. "And what's her, uh, issue?"

I give a subconscious shake of the head, then catch myself.

I look back at Mark.

Realise I can't lie to him.

Or, at least, I can't lie to him about *this* . . .

"Some family trouble," I say, "she lives with her father, but he just kicked her out."

Mark scowls. "Doesn't sound fair." He glances back at me. "Does she have some problems with drink, drugs?"

I shake my head. "No, it's a little . . . I don't . . ." I know that I'm going to have to put the whole truth to him, and nothing but ". . . her father just found out that she's not *his*, that somebody else fathered her."

That statement seems to strike Mark cold.

"That sounds so *cruel*," he finally gets out.

"I know," I reply, hoping this'll be the end of the conversation.

For a long while, the two of us sit up there, on the log, staring into the embers of the campfire.

Nothing to say.

"Anna?" he says, turning into me, and dropping his voice down to a whisper so that we won't be overheard by the children in their tents nearby, "I'm not Nathan's biological father, but I've not go around . . . it's just that there's never been the time, and then, my wife, she . . . ." Marks throat seems to seal up on him; he stays quiet for several moments, and then adds, "Do you think that I should, you know, *tell* him?"

I feel my heart pounding in my chest.

I only really came here on this training trip on a whim, I didn't want to end up having to dispense *advice* . . . but there doesn't seem to be any way around it now.

"Yes," I say, "after what I've seen—what Amy's gone through —I think he deserves to know the truth."

When I look back into Mark's eyes, I see that they're glittering with tears. He reaches up, wipes them away, then feeds me a hardy smile. "You know, if this hired-killer business ever falls through you'd make a great therapist."

Wow, was he ever telling the truth when he said he knows nothing about me . . .

Chapter Nineteen

E VERYBODY'S ALL SLEEPY when we get the car all
packed up following lunch the next day.

And it's no surprise, really.

That morning, we all slouched on a river bank and watched
on as Nathan and Ben set about attempting to cobble a raft
together out of large blue plastic barrels and pieces of twine; all
under the watchful eye of their coach, barking orders at them.

If Nathan and Ben achieved anything at all in terms of team-
work then I can't say that I observed it . . . I suppose those sorts
of things are better left to the experts.

The ones who *charge* for these things.

About half an hour away from the campsite, we celebrate
returning to civilisation with pizza all around. I go with ham and
pineapple, simply because I feel like I've short-changed my body
on fresh fruit and veg during the weekend and it seems the only
slightly healthy option in this salt-fest of ours.

Back in the car, everybody's quiet, and when I glance into the back seat, I see that all three kids are conked out. I look to Mark, who's driving along, his hair drawn back into a ponytail to stop it floating into his eyes. I make out the deep, black circles beneath each of his eyes and can tell that he didn't sleep much the night before.

I suppose it had something to do with our little chat around the campfire.

Neither of us speak.

First of all, we drop off Ben and Josie at Arnold's house.

I don't really feel like I can tell Mark to drive off before they let themselves in through the front door which maximises the possibility of an awkward meet-and-greet situation.

Thankfully, though, Ben gets his key in through the keyhole, and he and his sister disappear inside, with a pair of quick waves to us out in the car.

I suppose that Josie's looking forward to getting back to her clean linen, and a shower; while Ben is chomping at the bit to plug himself into his latest videogame, whatever that is.

Once we get going again, I glance over my shoulder, into the back seat, and Nathan smiles back at me.

As Nathan turns to look out the window, tracing the foliage as it passes by, I wonder if Mark's going to have the conversation I *advised* him to have the night before.

It could *very well* all blow right up in my face.

And I can't say that I'm all that eager for that to happen.

Once we arrive back to my house, and under Nathan's watchful gaze from the back seat, I give Mark a peck on the cheek then go around to gather up my hard-shell suitcase and day bags from the boot.

A cursory look over my house reveals that everything's in order.

Or *seems* to be.

No broken windowpanes.

The front door seems to be secure.

The only notable absence, and I don't notice this until Mark has driven off away up the road, is that there's no sign of AA's car parked up on the curb:

The sleek, black estate is notable by its absence.

As I lug my two day bags—one over either shoulder—and wheel my hard-shell case behind me up the garden path, I wonder if AA's already totalled the car.

That does bring out a slight smile on my lips.

I hope he had good insurance . . .

I turn the key in my front door, and step on in over the threshold.

I call out into the house.

No reply.

I sniff the air; half expecting to catch a whiff of dead bodies —*something* like that—but it all smells vaguely of disinfectant, as if somebody's had a quick whip around with a mop and bucket.

I don't think I can complain about that.

I set my bags down in the hall, and take a few steps into the house.

That's when I hear the whimpering *miaow, miaow, miaow* coming from the kitchen.

I go to check what's up with that.

Lizzie leaps from one of the kitchen chairs, trots up to me, rubs her body against my leg and continues her loud protest.

I glance over to her food bowl, in the corner of the kitchen.

See that it's empty.

I tread over the kitchen tiles—the *clean* kitchen tiles—and say, half to myself, and half to Lizzie, "Has nobody fed you yet?"

Lizzie yowls, apparently in reply.

I deal with the cat-food situation.

Get Lizzie all fed, and then set about on a proper investigation of the house.

All Amy's belongings—which is to say the clothes I leant-slash-gave to her are all in the chest of drawers. When I touch her towel, it's still damp.

So she was at least here this morning.

Finally it hits me.

I rush back down the stairs, to one of the daypacks.

After a brief dig about the pockets, I uncover my phone.

I toddle back upstairs, find my phone charger, right where I left it before the camping trip, sitting in a snake of cable on my bedside table.

Hands shaking all over the place, I plug the charger into the wall.

Inject the metal contact into the bottom of the phone.

The screen blinks to life—awash with a bluish light.

I tap my foot as I wait, impatient for the damn thing to find some signal.

While I wait, Lizzie wraps herself about my legs, giving me a grateful spate of *purrs* . . . no doubt *educating* me that feeding the cat in a timely manner is very much the Right Thing to do.

The network provider appears on the screen.

I wait another moment longer.

The messages hum into my palm.

Ten of them.

I work quickly, going through the options, scanning the senders.

There're several from AA.

Amy decided, in the interest of not leaving a trace, to ditch her phone soon after leaving her home . . . her *father's* home.

Quickly, I go through the list of messages which AA has sent me.

In a flurry of giddy thought, I wonder if there're enough messages there to turn into a novel.

I skim through the content, trying to decipher.

They're all mind-numbingly annoying messages like:

Had dinner. Pasta and pesto. Tasted great!

Or:

Taking her out for a walk. Thought she could use the exercise. Might want to take a leaf out of her book yourself, chubby buns.

I overlook the insult for the time being.

I flip through the other messages, finally find the last one he sent.

The one he sent a couple of hours ago:

Going out for a drive. Back later.

AA xx

I stare at the screen of my mobile phone for a long while, absorbing the significance of the message. Has AA been given the order? Has Brian told him that he needs to 'take care' of Amy?

My mind runs at a thousand miles a minute as I bluster about the house, trying to overturn some sort of a clue, something which'll let me know *where* they are.

But nothing.

I dig out the rain-damaged diary—now bone-dry, but its pages all beginning to flake—from its place in the kitchen drawer.

At least AA didn't take *that.*

I slip the diary into my pocket, almost not thinking about it.

I hover over the kitchen table for a long few moments, and then decide there's nothing to be done. That I can't put it off any further.

I attempt to give AA another few calls, and then, unable to get through, I send the following message:

Where've you gone? Why??

That done, I examine myself in the mirror, think about whether it'd be totally appropriate to leave the house without changing out of the waterproof trousers I've worn for the last three straight days, and then realise that, really, there's no time.

I throw an overcoat about my shoulders.

Slip out the door.

To go and see Brian Mathewson.

Chapter Twenty

THE DOUBTS ONLY BEGIN to creep in when, in the back of a black cab, I feel my mobile phone vibrate in my pocket: Brian's message back to me.

He gives me his home address, where he hides out in his spare time; where he is when he's not in his office, or abroad on business. The address he gives me is a little way across town, in Wimbledon.

It can be fairly assumed that he'll be well-cut.

Nothing quite worth celebrating like the weekend.

Not to mention his daughter's death.

The taxi driver looks a little confused when we pull up at a leafy, little suburban park, vacant except for a group of four teenagers; all of them wearing tracksuits, baseball caps pulled way down over their faces, the orange glow of the ends of their cigarettes.

They sit on a swing set, their laughter cruel and twisted, and punctuated by them spitting at their feet.

The taxi driver eyes me in his rear-view mirror. "You sure about the address, love?" he says, his voice coming through the speaker in the back seat.

I feel a slight wince at the term of endearment and not a little intimidated that, if this taxi driver decides to get 'sleazy,' there'll be nowhere to run to except for that park.

And its delinquents.

I look back to the screen of my mobile phone, then I hold up the map so that he can see it through the clear, plastic window separating the front and back seats.

Frown lines appear in his forehead. He scrutinises the houses on our right-hand side.

Shakes his head.

"Nah, somebody's having you on, love. Not here, this ain't the place. You reckon the house number is right, or what?"

I check the number again.

Number thirteen.

What *is* it with Brian and *that* particular number . . .

It's then, my finger flipping through my list of recently dialled numbers, ready to tap Brian's name, when I hear the sharp *rap* of knuckles against the back window of the cab.

At *my* window.

I turn to look, see that, standing there, is a dour-looking, skinny man in a suit.

Somewhat overdressed for a Sunday, at least for this century.

I glance to the taxi driver, who's looking back at me.

I can hear the taxi's engine still ticking over and, all of a sudden, the taxi driver doesn't look so sleazy after all.

"You know 'im, love?" he says, peering at the man outside my window.

I'm on the point of saying no when I give the man in the suit a second look over, decide that he looks well into his seventies, and is clearly not a threat to me.

For an assassin, I should be able to handle myself around a pensioner.

Famous last words . . .

"Here's fine," I say, and then shove one ten- and one twenty-pound note into the tray.

The taxi driver says nothing else.

Just takes my money.

I step out of the cab.

———

A chilly breeze blows along the pavement.

Here there're clear, white slabs of concrete.

A *pleasant* neighbourhood.

I draw the collar of my overcoat up, to cover my neck from the cold.

The man stands before me, his eyes so sunken into their sockets that they're almost nothing more than little black dots. He smells slightly of elderberries. His black suit is made of fine threads—which ones, I'm not exactly sure—and the white shirt he wears underneath brings out the walnut colour of his skin . . . that type of Caucasian skin that's been well-fried by a lifetime of summers. His black tie makes him seem like he's prepared for any occasion.

But especially a *funeral*.

The man gazes over the top of my head.

I listen to the *rumble* of the taxi engine leaving us behind.

My one means of escape.

Over, at the park, I hear a *cackle* of laughter from the delinquents.

That, more than the cool breeze, brings goose pimples rising up out of my skin.

"This way, please, madam," the man says, turning his back to me.

"Uh," I just about get out, then realise that the man's abrupt pace along the leaf-strewn pavement is leaving me behind, "just *who* are you . . . what's going *on* here?"

The man paces on, and I can tell, even from barely seeing his face in profile, that he's smiling slyly.

It makes me want to give him a punch.

If only he wasn't a septuagenarian . . .

Without so much as a muttered word in response to my polite enquiry, he leads me around the bend, along the pavement.

He seems to know where he's going.

Finally, he comes to a standstill beside a—*somewhat unremark-able*—grisly-grey hatchback car, parked up between a pair of, very sleek-looking, estate cars with tinted windows. From the inside pocket of his jacket, he produces a key fob and, with a movement that's too fast for me to even process, he taps the button.

The car's hazard lights blink in unison.

Twice.

A tiny, almost imperceptible, *pip* of the horn.

The man rounds the car, opens the driver's door.

I decide that *here* is the point where I need to be certain.

"Brian Mathewson?" I say. "You're taking me to see Brian?"

The man's smile bends the wrinkles around his eyes, softening them, making his withered, thin face seem a lot more wholesome . . . still, despite the smile, he's ten or so kilos off being a jolly, old 'grandpappy.'

"Yes, madam," he replies, then indicates my side of the car.

I eye him for a long few moments, glance up the street.

See one of those youths glaring back at me.

I get into the car.

———

The journey takes much longer than I expect.

For some reason, I always believed that Brian lived inside the city, but, from this experience, I suppose not.

I notice—because I have a paranoid mind attuned to noticing such things—that the man driving glances up into the rear-view mirror far more often than recommended by the Highway Code. One of these times, I glance back over my shoulder too and think to say, "Worried somebody might be following?"

The man just feeds me that same smile.

And we drive on.

———

The bizarre portion of the drive comes when the man pulls to one side of the motorway, into the hard shoulder.

For a couple of seconds, I wonder if he's caught a flat, and look out the window.

It's dark now—night-time—so I can't really tell.

But, soon enough, I find out that it's not to check for a flat tyre.

The man checks his rear-view mirror *again*, and then he reaches into the back seat of his car. He produces, from one of the passenger foot wells, a canvas, black bag.

For the longest time, I stare at it. "What's that for?" I say, even feeling like a complete idiot as the words leave my mouth.

"Your telephone, madam."

"My . . ." I just about get out, before clocking just what is going on.

I dig about in the pocket of my waterproof trousers, now feeling *extremely* underdressed with this suited man sitting beside me. I slip out my mobile, hand it over into the driver's leather-gloved hands. He's produced a clear, zip-lock bag from some-where, and he drops my phone neatly inside, bringing the zip shut without a sound.

"If you wouldn't mind, my dear," he says, handing the bag to me.

"Over my head?" I say, my eyebrows making good progress into my hairline.

"Yes, please."

I look to the black, canvas bag, wondering to myself if it's not too late for me to back out of this whole deal. To just tell him that I can wait till Monday to see Brian . . . at Mathewson Media. And that's when I see, large, and impossible to miss, the black van with tinted windows pull up behind the man's hatchback.

I look back to the man, half expecting him to have pulled a gun on me.

Instead, though, he wears the same neutral expression from before, and he looks out ahead of him, one hand lightly resting on the steering wheel.

I breathe in once.

Twice.

On the third breath, I just *do it*.

I loosen the cord around the open end of the bag, bring it down over my head, and then, using the same cord, tighten it about my neck.

"Very good, madam," the man says, and then I hear my door click open.

I can't help thinking about how Brian Mathewson treats his houseguests little better than hostages, as I sit on a metal bench in the back of the van. No seatbelt, and so I feel every last one of the corners we take. Thankfully they didn't think to tie up my hands, so I can cling to the edge of the bench and prevent myself from tumbling forwards . . . and no doubt breaking a nail, if not something worse, like a *nose*.

The air in the van smells a *lot* like disinfectant, and I wonder to myself if there's some quite odious reason for that . . . did Brian's last houseguest wet themselves in here?

Or worse?

I've put off those scatological thoughts when, after a long pause, and the mechanical grinding of an electric motor—an automatic gate?—the terrain passing beneath the van changes from slick asphalt to flaky gravel.

I listen to the gravel ping up against the base of the van.

And, a couple of times, I'm worried that a hole might open up in the floor beneath my feet.

Thankfully it doesn't, though.

I only realise how dark it is inside the back of the van when the doors open and I feel harsh light layer itself against the canvas of my hood.

"My goodness, Anna, you do realise you could've taken then hood *off* once you got into the van, didn't you?"

Brian.

Chapter Twenty-One

THE MEN LEAD ME out from the van, and across the gravel drive.

Contrary to what Brian's said, not one of them seems to suggest that I can remove the hood. And I don't hear anything more from Brian for the time being.

I think I prefer it like that.

Not knowing.

What is it they say about ignorance and bliss?

When the crunching of gravel beneath my feet gives way, I find myself walking along concrete slabs. Those concrete slabs, in turn, give way to softer, more easily trodden, wooden floorboards.

I'm vaguely aware of crossing a threshold

The warmth up against my cheeks.

A door shutting at my heels with an efficient *snap*.

In the near distance, I can smell onions and garlic cooking.

That makes my stomach grumble a touch.

No time for dinner yet.

I feel a—surprisingly *firm*—grip take hold of my hand, and guide my own fingers up to the cord of my hood. It's strange how just having something over my head takes away most of my sense of space. I get my fingertips under the hem of the hood.

Tug it off.

I see Brian; wearing a pair of chequered cargo shorts, and a clean, untucked, blue shirt which stretches down well below his waistband. He has a drink in his hand.

A tumbler of whisky.

Almost totally depleted.

I judge from the current dilation of his pupils—not *too* bad—that he's still fairly coherent . . . far more coherent than he was during my *impromptu* visit to his office at Mathewson Media, in any case.

One thing the whisky seems to be working well on, though.

His *smile*.

He grins from ear-to-ear.

I run my fingers through my hair, glad to feel free once again.

To squeeze the tension out of my shoulders.

I glance about me, realise that I've arrived in what must be a sitting room. Just as I thought, the floorboards of the house have been left bare. There's a Persian rug draped across them, beneath the armchair-and-sofa set.

Off, in the corner of the room, I can see a calf-hide lamp shedding a bronze glow. Aside from a few candles, the fluorescent, white light which spills in from the kitchen, it's the *only* light.

It feels like I'm on the point of bursting.

I somehow manage to keep a hold on myself—keep myself *calm* enough to utter, "Amy—what're you going to do with Amy?"

If anything should knock that smile off his lips, it's *that* . . . but Brian continues to grin away, albeit with a slight squint of incomprehension. "Amy's fine, as far as I know," he replies, and then turns his back to me, makes his way to a room adjoining the sitting room, "How about a spot of dinner?"

———

For some reason, I always thought that Brian lived in some sort of unparalleled opulence. Now, though, coming to his house for the first time, and perhaps it's because of the lead-up—what with the cryptic pickup, the hood over the head, the van—but I was expecting something more.

The table is modest; a polished-up, rich chocolate-brown shade—rosewood? A pair of three-pronged candlesticks stand on the table. A pair of lamps sit in the corners, and they're turned down low. The wallpaper is a sort of gold-green pattern; and looks like it wouldn't be out of place in an old person's home.

Then again, what do *I* know about style?

There's probably enough room to seat four around the table . . . there're three of us now: me, Brian, and Brian's wife.

Brian's wife gave me a pleasant smile when I wandered in.

And not much else.

She wears a cream-coloured jumper with the collar of her blouse sticking up through the neck. The blouse is patterned with blue-and-white pinstripes. A string of pearls hangs down from her throat. The pearls bring out the pinkish glow of her cheeks.

A couple of times, Brian's wife glances up, casts a quick look over the table, doesn't quite meet my eye, and then returns to her food. After attempting to ask some polite questions—since I didn't *see* the garden, or even the *house* itself, I can't really comment on those—and since Brian's wife only feeds me mono-syllabic replies, I decide to give up trying.

On tonight's menu is salmon and rice.

I've never been much of a fish person, in fact I'm fairly convinced that I'm *allergic*, but I feel obliged to tuck in out of politeness . . . though why I'm bothering seems somewhat immaterial considering that I've come to throw a grenade at Brian's little family setup here.

With each bite, I wonder if Amy's dead.

If AA's finished her yet.

Every time I look up, I will Brian's wife from the dining room, but she remains where she is, patiently chewing through her dinner. Her silver cutlery catching the light which spills in from the doorway to the kitchen.

I notice the suited man, the elderly one who picked me up in the hatchback, standing to attention just inside the kitchen, ready to be called at a moment's notice.

I stare at his jacket for a little longer than is strictly subtle, trying to ascertain whether or not he's wearing a gun.

I would've thought—from his sticklike figure—that it wouldn't be difficult to spot.

And I can't *see* one at all.

Once we've finished with the salmon dish, and with me feeling a vaguely swollen sensation creeping its way up my throat, probably from the aforementioned allergy to seafood, the three of us sit back and watch on as Brian's butler—because I suppose that's what the elderly man who picked me up in the hatchback *is* —collects up the plates and cutlery and then slips off into the kitchen.

Brian claps his hands together.

The sound makes me flinch.

I look across the table, see that Brian's wife clutches her hands together, rests them on her placemat, and stares at them, as if entranced.

"Dessert?" Brian says, grinning at me.

I feel almost as if I'm bursting . . . as if I'm *going* to burst.

But, at the same time, I know that I've come here for Amy.

With an uneasy look across to Brian's wife, during which she meets my eye, she seems to catch onto the hint that there's business to be done here. She rises up from her seat, pads over to Brian, delivers a loveless kiss onto his left cheek and then mumbles something about having a headache—about heading up to *bed*.

When me and Brian are alone, I fix my glare onto him, and say, "Where's Amy?"

Brian continues to smile back at me.

His butler returns.

I glare at him.

Try my best to make him feel *unwelcome* here.

I could do *without* an eavesdropper, no matter how professional . . .

He *doesn't* get the hint.

"Perhaps a coffee, sir?" the butler says, then looks at me.

Brian nods along, flurries a hand over his head. "Yes, yes, that'll be fine."

The butler feeds me a slender smile as he slips through the doorway to the kitchen, and I can't help wondering if he's been tasked—by Brian's wife—to attempt to curtail Brian's drinking.

Isn't coffee what you give to drunks, to sober them up?

Brian breathes in deeply. He rocks his shoulders back. He gives a slight shake of his head, still smiling. "I thought that you had come here tonight—had gone to such great lengths to pay me a visit, because you had something to add to our previous conversation."

For several moments, I'm lost . . . I can't recall what I had for breakfast this morning, let alone anytime further back than that.

I guess it's been a long day.

Brian arches an eyebrow. He takes a sip from his glass of whisky, still eyeing me. He sets the glass down on the table—now empty. "Your retirement?"

I'd forgotten about it entirely.

I shake my head at my own scatterbrainedness. "No," I say, "there's not really anything to discuss in terms of that."

Brian gives a stiff nod. He considers his empty glass, as if he's thinking to himself about filling it again. In retrospect, the butler, and the *coffee*, arrive just in time.

I watch on as Brian observes the thick, black liquid trickle into the porcelain mug with an expression which might be suitable for a dictator—his people at the gates with pitchforks—preparing to slug back poison.

The butler serves me coffee too.

I breathe in the rich scent, lay a hand against the mug.

Feel the warmth against my skin.

I take a sip.

Feel the hot coffee scald my tongue.

Its bitter flavour bite my tonsils.

I turn my attention back onto Brian. "There's something you have to know about Amy," I say, "something important, something that you might not have considered."

"Oh?" Brian says, staring into his coffee, apparently having no intention of taking so much as a sip. He turns to look at me. "And what's that?"

"She's your daughter."

Chapter Twenty-Two

F OR THE FIRST TIME in the entirety of our relationship, I have the pleasure of observing Brian Mathewson being stumped.

Oh, he does his best to hide it.

He continues to stare down into his coffee, head cocked slightly to one side; that faint smile still clinging to his lips as if *I'm* the one on the back foot here.

Finally, he looks at me, then says, succinctly, "*Explain.*"

I reach for the diary, still snug in the pocket of my waterproof trousers. I wonder if I should show it to him, if it would be breaking Amy's trust to show it to him. But I reason with myself that Amy's life is on the line and I must do everything in my power to keep her from harm.

Now Brian's expression *does* shift its course. He furrows his brow. "Is that . . ." he just about gets out of his lips, then turns his attention to me. "How did you . . ."

I hold so tight to the diary that it might as well be a life raft, the only thing keeping me afloat at sea. "Amy," I say, "she gave it to me—and *her* mother gave it to *her*."

Brian nods to himself, as if explaining the situation to his own mind.

Trying to connect the dots.

All those years ago.

He reaches out to me, for the diary.

I hold back for a few seconds then realise, having come this far, that there's nothing I can do to keep him from seeing the diary now.

It'd only weaken my position.

Only weaken *Amy's* position.

My hands tremble a little as I pass the diary over to him, though, for the love of all things holy I can't tell why . . . do I really think that Brian Mathewson's going to have me killed here, in his *own* home?

Then again, my instincts have been telling me to keep an eye on the butler . . . too many clichés *not* to keep an eye on the butler . . .

Brian wrinkles up his nose as he inspects the diary in his hand. He glances at me briefly. "Looks like it's been out in the rain."

"Mm," I reply, "occupational hazard of being in an assassin's care."

Brian doesn't smile at my joke—in actual fact, I don't think that he hears it at all. He flips through the water-damaged pages which look more like a thousand-year-old manuscript that's been dug up in the back garden rather than a diary which is barely a couple of decades old.

I watch on as he turns to the first page, to that little inscription of his.

Apparently finished with his inspection, he breathes out a long, hard sigh, then looks over at me, meeting my gaze. "All right," he says, "how much d'you want for it?"

My stomach dips as I consider the implications of this.

Does he *care* that he has a daughter?

Is he concerned about somebody else finding out . . . his *wife* finding out that he knowingly had his daughter murdered?

"I . . . *nothing*," I finally reply. "I just wanted to let you know."

" 'To let me know,' " Brian replies, staring at the diary in his hand, transfixed by it, and his thoughts clearly in another place.

"Brian?" I say. "Where is she?"

Brian remains sitting still. He doesn't appear to hear me.

I get up out of my chair.

Tread over to him.

Take hold of his upper arm in a vice-like grip.

He still doesn't look at me.

Doesn't seem to *notice* me at all.

"It can all be over now," I say, "you *don't* need to do this."

Brian holds himself still another few moments, staring at the cover of the diary—the *date* there—and then he drops it down on his placemat. "Thank you for telling me this, Anna," he says.

"You're welcome," I say, my tone of voice deadpan.

I release him from my hold.

I sense that the butler has arrived at my heels.

That he's keeping a close watch on my movements.

He has a gun pointed at the back of my head, for all I know.

"Now will you let her go?" I say.

Brian turns the diary over in his hands. "Can I keep this?"

"Yes," I say, feeling the blood pump to my temples.

At any given moment, I feel a hair away from breaking out into violence.

And what frightens me the most about the feeling is that I don't know if I'll be able to stop it. Because once I've flipped my Kill Switch, it's all over.

Everything's over.

Brian leans his head back to me. "I don't know where she is, Anna, I have no idea. All that I know is what Charlie Branwick, her . . ." I feel the unspoken word lodge in his throat now that he realises the truth . . . "what he told me, that she's disappeared. That he wanted my help to find her . . ."

My ears perk up to hear mention of Charlie Branwick; Brian's good, old buddy.

The Cold Case *Club*.

"What did you tell him?" I say.

"That I'd do my best—put my ear to the ground, that sort of thing."

I feel a numbing sensation crawl all over my skin now.

It feels impossible to stop.

"And?" I say, my voice catching in my throat.

Brian stays still for the longest time, then he shakes his head. "No, I had no idea. She just disappeared. She knew what she was doing."

"You didn't know that she was staying with me?"

I round the table, unable to believe this.

Finally, on the other side of the table, I press the heels of my hands down onto the slick, polished-up surface, stare right back into Brian's eyes. "You're telling the truth—you *really* didn't know."

Brian breaks off my gaze, turns his attention back down to the diary sitting on the placemat before him. "Nobody can know *everything*, Anna."

Chapter Twenty-Three

BRIAN WON'T ALLOW ME to leave that night, to go and search for Amy. But he assures me—when I ask again, and *again*—that he had nothing to do with ordering AA to take care of Amy. As he points out to me, even before he found out the truth, that she's his daughter, he wouldn't have had any *reason* to do so . . . other than the fact that she was a minor annoyance, not a particularly good assassin, a standard case of friends trying to help one another's offspring out.

He puts me up in one of the guest rooms. It has an en suite, and a queen-sized bed. French doors leading out onto a balcony, which, when I attempt to turn one of the handles, I see have been nailed shut.

Well, a *fancy* prison cell, at least.

Breakfast is Continental:

Sliced, wholemeal toast. Buttered.

Granola. Milk.

More coffee.

I have to admit that I've never been much of a breakfast person—*it's all about the dinner*—but I find myself somewhat ravenous at the prospect.

Perhaps it has something to do with getting kidnapped.

Or *close to it*.

I say goodbye to Brian at around eight thirty, and I'm taken through the same old routine from last time, though, *unlike* last time, the hood isn't put over my head until I'm actually seated in the van. This gives me a chance to take a look at Brian's house.

Much more modest than I would've imagined.

Apart from its location, surrounded by bustling, leafy trees, and—apparently—countryside for miles around—the house itself is distinctly ordinary.

Three, maybe four, bedrooms.

A double garage.

The driveway *is* substantial.

And the house *is* a long way back from the road.

But, as I trundle away, blindfolded again in the back of the van, I can't help thinking to myself about how I'm a touch let down by how Brian lives.

Last year, when I stayed in his mansion in Spain, I caught a glimpse of his opulent lifestyle—and a whole bunch else—and I'd sort of expected to see it translated back to Blighty.

Maybe I'm not as good at reading people as I thought.

There you go, Anna Harris, noted sociopath: rubbish at reading people.

This time, instead of stopping on a hard shoulder of a motorway, the black van leaves me in the middle of a country lane. For a couple of seconds, as I stand there on the single-lane, very *empty* looking road, I wonder if I've been stitched up—if Brian is dealing me some sort of punishment for *demanding* to see him; if he's going to force me into the indignity of walking home.

Right as I turn to ask one of the expressionless men in suits who drive the van, I notice the plain, battered hatchback parked up behind. I give the men in suits a parting smile then round the van, see that the butler is back behind the wheel.

———

It's hard to say whether the butler is more or less talkative than the first time . . . but it's a fact that he doesn't say very much at all.

This time, instead of taking me back to that address in Wimbledon, he drops me off at the end of the Underground line in Morden. Right as I'm on the point of getting out of his car, he stops me with a slight touch on my forearm.

This is the moment I'd feared.

I brace myself as he reaches for the glove compartment.

Ready to act if necessary.

I tell myself, over and over again, that this man is at least in his seventies, and that I can overpower him if I absolutely *have* to.

I look about, through the windscreen, to the many people wandering about the façade of the station. Too many witnesses. It'd be impossible. Even Brian would have a tough time putting a positive spin on one of his employees filling a car with a bloody cloud in bright daylight, in the middle of a busy centre of activity.

However, from within the glove compartment, the butler slips out my mobile phone. All nice and wrapped up in its zipped, transparent plastic bag.

I give an internal sigh, take it from him, then thank the butler, for all the good it seems to do.

Seemingly the second I step out of his car, he guns the throttle and pulls out of the car park. As I walk towards the station building, already wondering what it might've cost the butler to drive me *all* the way home, I jab the Power button on my mobile.

Wait for it to load up.

I've already navigated through the crowded station floor, breathed in a good amount of that oily smell—that clammy *feel*—which seems to accompany all stations in the city, and got myself to an automatic ticket machine before I think to check my mobile-phone screen again.

One new message.

I tap.

From AA:

We're somewhere safe, somewhere far away from you.

My blood runs cold.

I try to decipher—*precisely*—what he means.

Realise that there can't be any other explanation.

He's afraid.

Afraid of *me*.

———

It takes just over an hour for me to get back home, and when I do Lizzie is yowling her head off again. I suppose that my indiscipline with her feeding regime *has* been vaguely outrageous these last few days. I get the cat fed, and she thanks me kindly.

Next of all, I search through the house, trying to turn up any sort of clue that Amy might still be there, but everything seems just as I left it.

Unable to think of anything else to do, I put the kettle on.

I stand at my kitchen window.

Waiting.

Listening to the kettle froth away to itself.

Begin to *bubble*.

It's when I look out of my kitchen window—into the *street*—that I see them.

Three men, all of them bulky.

All of them wearing long overcoats.

At first, I'm certain that they're bouncers, all on their way to work, chewing things over together as they think about a long night ahead . . . but then one of them glances up, looks over my house.

To my front door.

To the *number* on my front door.

He nudges the one behind him. And then all three of them are staring.

I know I have seconds.

Seconds.

Leaving the boiling kettle behind, pluming searing-hot steam into the air, I dash up the staircase, trying to make as little noise as possible, and *surely* failing.

I get up to my bedroom, to my wardrobe.

I search through my things, to the cardboard box I keep within.

Where I stash all my tools of the trade.

I drag it along my bedroom carpet.

Tear the lid as I rip it free.

Then I peer inside.

Nothing.

There's *nothing* there.

No gun.

At my front door, I hear the *thud-thud-thud* of knuckle against wood.

Quickly, my mind switches to the .32 I keep down in the hallway.

But already something's fired in my brain.

I know that searching there will be in vain.

AA took my guns.

And he'll have taken the one downstairs *too*.

I hear muttering on my front doorstep.

When I crawl out onto the landing, peer through the wooden railings of the banister, down to the front door, I can see their forms through the frosted glass.

Lizzie emerges from God-knows-where, she sniffs at the air.

Stares up at the frosted glass.

At the figures obscured beyond it.

What must be going through her cat brain . . . what's going through my *human* brain?

I launch myself back up onto my feet, rush back into my bedroom, look down into my back garden where, sure enough, one of the men in overcoats has appeared. He's reaching inside his jacket. His eyes constantly on the move. Looking for any sort of motion at all.

Ready to draw his weapon.

It's only when I hear Lizzie let out an elongated *hiss* down in the hallway that I realise there's just one way out of the house now.

I look over to Amy's room—what *was* Amy's room.

The window.

Overlooking the side alley.

The one which peers right into my neighbour's attic bedroom.

Into Mrs Pietersen's bedroom.

Chapter Twenty-Four

I MANAGE TO GET MYSELF out through the window; and onto the roof, the second I hear my front door creaking open. I would've thought that I'd forgotten to lock up if it hadn't been for the giveaway *clickety-click* of lock-picking going on.

With a quick glance down into my back garden, to see the third member of the trio looking through my French doors, and through the living room to the front door; I leap the metre-or-so gap over to Mrs Pietersen's roof.

In mid-air, I mumble a little prayer, hoping both not to make a sound and to land safely on the other side. From what I hear, breaking a leg—*as an assassin*—is really not advisable in terms of future job prospects.

Although I feel one of the roof tiles loosen a little beneath the sole of my boot, I have the presence of mind to stomp down hard, to keep it in place.

Heart in my mouth, I glance back over my shoulder, to the back garden.

To Goon Number Three.

It's that moment when one of the other goons, inside the house now, unlocks the French doors, slides them back, and welcomes his mate in.

Just make yourself at home.

As I stare on at my house, clinging to the roof, one leg dangling down below me to give me some sort of support, I consider my next move.

I glance to the window of Mrs Pietersen's attic bedroom, then reach out for it, give it a shove inwards.

Nope.

No movement.

I suppose she's more wary about her *own* personal security.

About who *she* goes around handing her keys out to.

I press my face up against the glass and, holding my hand over my eyes to shield the glare of daylight, I peer inside.

Well, the room *looks* empty.

Although I wouldn't consider myself a nosey neighbour, I have to admit that I've been aware enough to realise that Mrs Pietersen is hardly ever present in this room. Only a couple of times that I've happened to be looking out of the window and seen Mrs Pietersen tending the bed, or cleaning up something or other.

I guess I've got to take the chance.

It's either that or jump.

And I can't quite see bending my knees keeping me from serious injury.

I wait for a long few seconds, though I'm not entirely sure why.

Then, pulling the sleeve of my fleece over my hand, I draw back a fist and punch the corner of the window:

Quick and *hard*.

The window is thin.

Not double-glazed.

I punch right through.

And I have the good sense to remind myself not to whip my arm back.

Not to slice up my nerves on the jagged glass.

I hold my hand still, now inside the attic bedroom.

With the other hand, I pick at the remaining shards of glass.

The pointy bits.

Then I reach for the latch, lying prone within.

I lift it up, and away.

Opening the window.

I lean out a little as I draw the window towards me.

Then, with a final look over my shoulder, I manoeuvre myself inside the attic bedroom.

Back to relative safety.

———

I quickly scope out the attic bedroom.

A bed pushed into one corner, with a patchwork quilt covering it.

I imagine that Mrs Pietersen's grandchildren—does she *have* grandchildren?—sleep here when they come to visit.

The room smells a little musky, and the dust lining the air tickles my nostrils and throat.

Just breathing in, I can almost taste the sugary goodness of the various brownies, and cookies, and whatever else it is that Mrs Pietersen cooks up.

I perk up my ears, listen for any sound in the house.

Hearing nothing, I turn back to the window.

Try to work out if the damage is noticeable from the outside.

Not particularly.

I was careful with that punched hole in the glass.

What *is* noticeable, however, is the fact that I left Amy's bedroom window wide open.

And that Lizzie, apparently having sniffed me out and attempting to follow me, is now crouched on the window ledge.

Eyeing up the jump.

She meets my eye for a second.

I tell her, in the clearest feline telepathy, *NO!* but it doesn't seem to do any good.

She takes a half step back and then leaps.

Lands with—well—*catlike* grace on the roof.

I reach out, lever the window open quickly, inviting her inside.

As I gather her in my arms, I can't help muttering, "You could've shut the window behind you on your way out, you know?"

But she only purrs at me.

Self-satisfied.

Lizzie rescued, I step out of range of the window—not wanting any of the men to spot me standing here, in my neighbour's house. Safe and sound.

When I turn around into the attic bedroom once more, I find myself standing almost nose-to-nose with Mrs Pietersen.

An extremely confused look on her face.

Chapter Twenty-Five

THE TWO OF US just stare at one another for a long while.

The air between us seems to tighten like a screw.

I have a good amount of time to take in Mrs Pietersen's appearance.

The shapeless, mauve dress she wears.

Pinny apron strapped about her waist.

Oven gloves dangling down from her left hand.

Before either one of us can say a word, though, there's a knock at the door.

We both look off in the direction of the front door.

Downstairs.

Who knows what she's thinking—but I know *exactly* what I am.

And I express that thought in clear, easy-to-understand words.

"Answer it," I say, meeting her eye as she turns back to me, "*Please.*"

I'm not sure whether it's because Mrs Pietersen is totally shell-shocked by the experience, or if she senses the desperation in my voice, but she slips out of the attic bedroom, quickly and without question.

Then she descends the stairs, goes to the front door.

I clutch Lizzie tight to my chest, feel her body warm, and purring.

She's just pleased with her display of high-altitude acrobatics.

She has no idea what sort of trouble we're in . . . but, to tell the truth, I don't have much of an idea *either*.

Downstairs, I listen to Mrs Pietersen speak with the men at the door.

From what I can hear—nothing much more than their grumbling, drawling voices—they sound as if they're being polite, as if they're treating Mrs Pietersen just as they would treat any other elderly stranger whose door they happened to knock on.

I press my back up against the wall of the attic bedroom, turn my attention to the ceiling, and pray for the men to just go away. For what Mrs Pietersen says to them to make them go away.

Finally—*mercifully*—I hear the front door click shut downstairs once again.

Then Mrs Pietersen's gentle footsteps sounding on the staircase.

She returns to the doorway.

Places a hand on her hip. "Those men said they're the police."

"Did they?" I say my voice sounding flimsy—*weak*. "What did you tell them?"

A slight smile twitches at the corner of her mouth. "They

asked if I'd noticed any odd sounds, asked if there was anybody else in the house."

"And what did you say?"

"I said that I was the only person here."

I allow myself a cleansing exhale. "Thank you," I just about get out.

"Come on, then," she says, turning to leave the attic bedroom, "I just put the kettle on—you can tell me all about it."

I feel as if I'm going to faint.

————

Thankfully, Mrs Pietersen's kitchen doesn't have a window which looks out into the street. It looks out into her back garden, which, I can't help noticing, is in a *far* better state than my own. I must get the number of her gardener once this is all over.

Presuming that I'm still alive.

I'm trembling as I sit down at Mrs Pietersen's kitchen table, Lizzie still clutched in my grasp. Only when Lizzie gives me a little nibble do I realise that I'm squeezing the life out of her. I let my arms go loose and she bounces down off my lap, onto the kitchen floor.

As the kettle boils away, I take in the pleasant kitchen tiles: the stencilled farm tools; and the wheat colour scheme. I have to admit that Mrs Pietersen certainly knows how to make a house a home . . . perhaps I should've brought a notepad and pencil.

"So," Mrs Pietersen says, bringing my steaming cup of tea over, "about those men—*the police?*"

I feel a tingle run up my spine.

When I look over Mrs Pietersen's expression, I see her

plucked eyebrows bowing into one another, the wrinkles in her forehead growing deeper.

"Were they police?" she says.

I give a shake of my head, look to Lizzie, who's sniffing about Mrs Pietersen's kitchen floor. It's then that I notice her go over to a food bowl, a few dry biscuits there, and she sets about munching on them quite happily. "I don't know who they are," I say, answering as honestly as I can at this moment in time.

I would protect Mrs Pietersen from the truth . . . if I knew what the truth *was*.

Together, we eye Lizzie at the food bowl.

Mrs Pietersen gives a sigh. "She's over here most days," she says, "first time she came over was about a week after my own cat, Monsieur Stripy"—I don't think to question the name right now—"passed away." A slight smile springs up on her lips. "Funny how I never thought to empty out his food bowl—just never occurred to me." She turns to look at me. "And then, one day, just like that, this pretty little girl pops through the cat flap, starts stuffing her face with his food."

Lizzie crouches down on her haunches, clearly content to be chewing her way through the food.

I had noticed that Lizzie was getting a little dumpy around the tummy, but I thought it was just some sort of middle-aged cat thing.

"Sorry," I say, meeting Mrs Pietersen's eye for a brief second.

Mrs Pietersen, still smiling, bats her hand and says, "No, I like to have the company." She looks back over to Lizzie. "Nice to have visitors every now and again."

I can't shake the feeling that this last comment is directed at me.

And it's true . . . I almost never come over unless it's to break through an attic window.

Mrs Pietersen, having hovered over the table, clutching her cup of tea the entire time, finally squats down onto one of the chairs. She takes a sip, then says, "You know, dear, you can tell me just what's going on with those men, you can *trust* me, I can be a friend."

I look back into Mrs Pietersen's eyes, Lizzie's constant masticating providing an aural backdrop to this touching moment.

Mrs Pietersen reaches across the table, presses her lips tightly together, as if considering something closely, and then says, "Is it something to do with a man?"

" 'A man?' " I say tilting my head to one side.

"Yes, you know," she goes on, breaking off eye contact, "when things like this begin to happen there's often a *man* behind them."

I suppose that she's correct in her assumption.

Whoever sent those men, whoever those men *were*, I guess there's a good, fifty-percent probability, that another man is behind them.

"I . . ." I just about get out, "it's not what you think . . ."

But Mrs Pietersen holds up her hand and, before I can say anything further, she rounds the table, approaches me from behind and takes hold of me.

From the frantic past twenty-four hours, I can't help thinking that there's some sort of malice intended from this gesture. I get a hold of myself, snap my brain back to the idea that *normal* people act like this all the time; *normal* people often *enjoy* embracing others.

"You're safe now, dear," Mrs Pietersen says, her voice up against my ear now.

I can smell her perfume: it smells like something between pineapples and mint.

She's warm.

And, to be honest, I don't break off the cuddle right away, set her straight, because it's been a long time.

Sometimes you just need a hug.

"Let me tell you," Mrs Pietersen says, "the most important thing of all is the first step . . . to just know when to *walk away.*" I hear her swallow hard, actually feel the movement of her throat against my neck. "But it's the best decision I ever made, because, who knows, if I'd stayed, I might not have lived to tell the tale."

Now I do shift a little in Mrs Pietersen's embrace, so that I can make out her eyes: round and caring, and obviously wanting to *help* me.

Her arms loosen on me, she seems to retreat, almost floating backwards.

Away from me.

"I'm so sorry," she says, "so *sorry* for giving him the key . . . it's just that, I thought, well, since I'd seen the two of you together; coming and going; that it wouldn't be an issue. I didn't want to be the annoying neighbour getting in the way."

It's then that my mind kicks in.

Tells me that Mrs Pietersen is thinking of AA as being some sort of *partner* of mine.

And, from the context of what she's saying, that she believes he's been *beating* me, or something to that effect.

"I want to show you something," Mrs Pietersen says, rolling up one of the sleeves of her dress.

I want to set her right, but it seems like this conversation has already got away from me.

She shows me her skin: slightly tanned, mottled with veins,

and moles, sagging a little off her bones. As she rolls the sleeve up further, I observe the scar coming into view.

Thick.

Red.

Shiny in the dim daylight which slivers into the kitchen.

And it keeps on going.

The scar *keeps on going*.

Finally, she brings her sleeve up to her bicep, to show me a scar that must be at least as long as a good-sized kitchen knife.

When I turn my attention from the scar, and back to her face, she says, "Anna, you've got to be the one to walk away—the one to make the first move . . . you don't want to let him be the one to dictate proceedings." She holds herself still, showing off that scar of hers. "Those men, those men *show* that he isn't enough of a man to face you himself, that he needs to have others along to intimidate, to stop you feeling safe."

Without another word, she rolls the sleeve of her dress back down.

Retakes her seat in the chair opposite me.

Looks down into her waiting cup of tea.

———

The air in the kitchen feels suddenly frosty.

My heart skips a few beats.

The floor beneath my feet seems unsubstantial.

But I keep myself together.

It seems almost in another world that I feel Lizzie brushing her head up against my leg.

I hear a faint buzzing in the distance. I realise eventually that it's one of the strip bulbs which hangs over the kitchen counter, shedding even light over the surface. My mouth tastes a little of blood, that image of Mrs Pietersen's terrible scar now emblazoned on my mind's eye. On impulse, I reach down, lift Lizzie up, bring her onto my lap. I breathe in her fur; that musky scent, thick with earth and leaves. A little piece of nature.

Mrs Pietersen nods to Lizzie, in my arms. "I can look after her," she says. "I can keep an eye on the house—and tell *him* where he can go when he comes back."

I feel my throat tighten now, and realise that I need to step in, that I need to *say* something here. ". . . No," I say, hardly croaking the word. "*No.*"

But Mrs Pietersen won't hear of it.

Already, she's up and over to the cordless phone which hangs in its cradle on the wall. She swipes it up, then consults a smorgasbord of pieces of paper pinned to the wall:

Phone numbers.

She dials.

Each button stroke emits a flat, obnoxious tone.

"It's for the best, Anna, believe me." She turns to look at me, gives me the hint of a smile. "I've been a volunteer with the Winged Women's Institute ever since *I* escaped . . ."

Just that name sends a shudder down my spine—I wonder what it means exactly.

Freedom?

" . . . They'll take care of you, keep you safe. You won't need to worry about him anymore."

I squeeze Lizzie all the tighter, feeling myself sinking down into my chair.

I wonder if I can go through with this.

If I can exploit a service like this.

Just to make my getaway.

The call takes a surprisingly short time.

Less than a couple of minutes.

Mrs Pietersen hangs the phone back up in its cradle. She rests that fist of hers on her hip, looks me over, gives me a faint smile, and then says, "They'll be here in half an hour—let's get you ready."

When she sees that this doesn't entirely console me that I'm, no doubt, still looking somewhat blindsided by this swift series of events, Mrs Pietersen draws close. She rests the heels of her hands on the table, spread an even shoulder-width apart. When she speaks again, it's in a husky whisper. "Don't worry, Anna, if the worst comes to the worst, upstairs"—her eyes swivel upwards, to the kitchen ceiling—"I've a gun."

———

'Getting ready' entails the Thelma-and-Louise routine:

Headscarf.

Wide sunglasses: they have a crack in them, but they'll do.

And a large overcoat, to conceal my body shape, I suppose.

Already, and standing in Mrs Pietersen's bedroom, before an enormous full-length mirror with a glistening silver frame, I look myself over.

I can't quite shake the feeling that I look *exactly* like some Hollywood star attempting to evade the paparazzi.

But Mrs Pietersen, here, appears to be the expert.

She looks on over my shoulder, fingers resting in the pit of her chin, head tilted *just so* to one side. She gives a nod of approval, looking to me, as if *I'm* going to have any sort of opinion on this.

When we get down in the front hall, I see, out the window,

that a large, white four-by-four with tinted windows is waiting. I can only make out the silhouette of the driver. Already, the October-afternoon light is fading.

I turn to Mrs Pietersen, and then to Lizzie, who has been ever-present throughout this entire wardrobing excitement. She pushes up against my leg and, feeling somewhat unwieldy in my getup, I reach down and take her in my arms.

After a brief cuddle, I hand her over to Mrs Pietersen.

Lizzie doesn't seem to have any issue with Mrs Pietersen holding her, which is more than can be said for the majority of the world's people.

"Take care, dear," Mrs Pietersen says. "They might still be out there—*watching.*"

I can't quite shift that feeling either.

In fact, I feel a slight tremor beneath the surface of my skin.

Almost as if some insect is burrowing through my veins.

Trying to *burst* out.

In a dead, grainy voice, I just about manage to mumble, "Thank you—thank you so much." And, as I step out the door, leaving my neighbour and cat behind, I can't help but think that it's as sincere an expression of gratitude as I can muster.

Just not for the reason that Mrs Pietersen believes.

————

I've hardly got into the back seat of the four-by-four, when the driver pushes the pedal to the floor, throwing me backwards before I've so much as had the opportunity to put on my seatbelt. As the driver, who I can only see the back of the head of, takes the corner at the end of my road, I manage—just about—to get buckled up.

We've driven on for about five minutes, and with the driver constantly checking the rear-view mirror, before the driver actually speaks to me.

Before *she* speaks to me.

"Outside your house," she says, "there were a couple of cars —neither seemed to recognise you, but you can never tell. Neither one of them's following us, anyway."

I glance back over my shoulder, look out through the rear window, and see—indeed—that there's nobody on our tail.

When I turn back to the front, I see the little pine-tree air freshener hanging from the rear-view mirror, and realise that's where the grassy, artificial smell is coming from. I study the driver in profile, the close-cropped, blond hair; the severe, hard-cut jaw.

Although I'm sure that the driver's a woman, I can't help thinking that there's something innately *masculine* about her appearance.

Perhaps it's the navy-blue men's jacket she wears, over a white shirt, and dress trousers.

Or how she wears the matching cap—the type worn by valets in films; the employees who tend to the mega rich . . . though this particular cap, despite having a gleaming visor, has several tears about its crown, as if it's been well-loved.

We drive on together, into the night.

Chapter Twenty-Six

I TAKE THE UNEXPECTED JOURNEY as an opportunity to catch up on some sleep, taking off my fleece—seeing as the car heaters are going at a heady rate—and bundling it up, to use as a makeshift pillow up against the window.

The gentle trundle of the car engine soon sends me drifting off.

We pull up with an abrupt *crunch* of tyres over gravel.

For a panicked few seconds, I glance about me, unable to see anything.

I wonder if—*somehow*—Brian has managed to get to me.

If he's had that same hood brought down over my face.

The car engine clicks off.

A door slams shut.

It's around that point when I realise that the fleece I'd been using as a pillow has slipped out of place and fallen down over my head.

I wrestle with it for a few seconds, cast it away, and then look up.

The inside of the car is lit with sallow lights.

I look to the front seat, see that the driver's no longer there.

I straighten up in my seat, padding my surroundings, trying to reassure myself that, really, I still exist within the real world.

I can hear low, drawling speech.

Outside the car.

I bend my neck, look out through the window.

The scene is lit by a bright, exterior light.

White light.

I see the driver standing there, a cigarette dangling from her fingertips, shedding smoke in upwardly curling spirals. She's speaking with another woman, dressed in a thick, woolly jumper, the sleeves of which are so long that they cover her hands.

The building which looms in the background brings to mind a sort of Victorian-style prison. It's ugly, square and—I think, but can't be sure because of the lack of daylight—that it's a dirty-brown shade. The windows are like narrowed, squinting eyes as if the building itself looks out upon the modern world and, in that very Victorian way, *disapproves*.

Some birch trees, low hedges which grow up around the building, soften the exterior a little. Make the place seem just a touch more homey.

I reach for the door handle, give it a firm tug.

The door opens and I slip out.

I'm surprised at how shaky my legs are when I stand up on the gravel driveway. I look to the driver and the woman in the jumper standing beside her; both of them are staring at me, the two of them with slightly amused expressions.

"Come on," the woman in the jumper says, approaching me, "let's get you a bed."

I have only a moment to murmur my thanks to the driver. She tosses her cigarette down on the gravel driveway and stamps it out with her heel, looks back at me and gives me that same smile. She tips her cap then gets back into the car.

As the woman in the jumper leads me towards the yawning jaws of the building's entrance up ahead, I hear the engine of the four-by-four snarl back into life.

———

Before I know it, my vision still bleary, my mind only half responding to the woman's friendliness, I find myself tucked up and asleep in a small room; only a camp bed, small bedside table and a lamp for company.

There's also one of those aforementioned, tight, squinting windows, through which the fledgling sunlight beams through onto my face, waking me. I lie there, listening to the birdsong, trying to figure out my precise location in the universe for several moments.

Finally, when I feel like I've got something of a handle on it, I shuffle out from underneath the sheets of the camp bed. I notice the pair of slippers resting beneath my camp bed.

Fluffy *white* ones.

I prod my feet into them and pad over to the window.

I can hardly see anything of the garden out of the window . . . mostly I can just see cars parked up at the front of the building: the white four-by-four among them.

Nobody walks around the gardens.

Something about this place makes me think of ghosts . . . and then I remind myself that I'm not eight years old any longer.

There's nothing in the drawer of the bedside table: only one of those cheaply produced bibles.

When I explore the room further, I find only a wardrobe: a well-dented, stainless-steel contraption which, I suppose, has suffered various, severe arse-kickings from Scout and Guide groups throughout the years.

Inside the wardrobe are about half a dozen coat hangers.

And a whole lot of dust.

In search of a toilet, I slip out through the wooden door to my room, and pad along the corridor. The floor of the corridor is that laminate-tiled stuff; that kind of texture which never fails to bring to mind hospitals, or school hallways.

I locate the toilet at the end of the hall, along with a mirror.

I'm a touch surprised to find, in the partially cracked, but ceiling-to-floor, mirror, that I'm wearing pyjamas: an off-white, V-necked top coupled with a pair of similarly coloured bottoms. I think about the last time that I wore pyjamas, and come to the conclusion that it must've been in the last century.

My skin seems a little grey in the light here, and, once I've made a quick toilet trip, I splash some water on my cheeks to wake me up.

When I return to my bedroom, I'm surprised to find the woman in the jumper from the night before standing there; a semi-transparent, pink plastic box at her feet.

I can see that, inside the box, are various items of clothing.

She gives me a smile, reaches out a hand for me to shake. "Hi there, Anna, remember me from last night? Georgie?"

I stare at her outstretched hand for several seconds, then take it off her.

Give it my best *firm* shake.

Georgie bends at the knees then picks up the box. "You mind getting the door for me, Anna?"

I do as she requests, then sit down on the edge of the bed as she sets the box down in the middle of the floor. She has fuzzy, puffed-up, brunette hair, and when some of it flurries into her mouth, she puffs it out again. When she straightens up, she hooks the offending portion of hair back behind her ear. I notice a gold-banded diamond on her ring finger. "So," Georgie says, "get a good sleep?"

"Uh," I say, hardly able to take my eyes off the box, "Yes, thank you." Then I look back to Georgie, unable to keep from asking the impertinent question. "Where're my clothes?"

"Ah," Georgie says, her mouth latched open, "they're being washed, for the time being, okay?"

I'm not totally sure I'm convinced of the simplicity of this statement.

I wonder if somebody's taking hair and skin samples off the clothes I came in, just in case I wish to press charges against my tormentor.

Against AA.

Georgie nods, as if to convince herself of her compact explanation, then turns her attention downwards to the box. "Brought some clothes along for you . . . until we can bring your own things here."

" 'My own things?' " I find myself repeating back at her, like some sort of android.

Georgie cocks her head to one side. "Sure, Anna, we'll have someone bring them here for you, so you don't need to go back."

I feel my stomach sink.

For some reason, I hadn't totally got a hold on just what I've got myself in for here . . . how I hoodwinked my neighbour into having me brought here, just so I could escape those 'men' . . .

"Now," Georgie says, meeting my eye—and I see that she has brilliant green eyes, "once you get yourself dressed and show-ered"—she slaps her forehead—"forgot the soap and towel, oh well—I'll be by again to take you down to breakfast. When you've got through with breakfast, you'll be seen by our in-house therapist, it's better that you talk about what happened, and *how* it happened with her, she's the one with the qualifications around here." Georgie pauses a moment, apparently to give me a moment to absorb that load of information. "Okay?" she says.

"Yes," I reply, then attempt a smile, "sounds . . . *good*."

"Great," Georgie says, and then heads for the door. "If you need anything at all, just give me a shout, all right? I'm only at the end of the hall." Right as she's about to slip out through the doorway, she sticks a finger up in the air, turns back to me with a slightly skittish expression, "The soap and towels, I'll be by to bring them in a moment or two." She presses on another smile. "You just get yourself comfortable, okay, Anna?"

"Fine," I say, "will do."

And with that, Georgie slips out of my bedroom.

Leaves me alone with the box of clothes.

———

With my towel wrapped around my waist, and smelling lightly of soap, I turn my mind to wardrobe.

After I've been digging through the box for about ten minutes, I finally turn up what seems—at least to my *inexpert* eye —to be something like an outfit.

A lime-green t-shirt with a cartoon cat on the front; a mean expression smeared on its face, and all its fur on end as it crouches protectively over its food bowl.

Beneath is the slogan:

No means no!

Then there's a pair of blue jeans—nothing much special about them, aside from the small tear at the crotch. I also pick out a bra and knickers, opting for the least soiled-looking, rather than attempting to coordinate the uncoordinateable.

They haven't seen fit to remove my boots from the vicinity, just having left them over in the corner of the room as if they're being punished for some reason. I loosen the laces and then push my feet inside. I think about how, only hours ago, I was wearing this same footwear out in the countryside with my kids; with *Mark*.

It's only then that I glance about me, searching for my mobile phone.

I turn my mind back to the night before, trying to jog my memory as to what I did with it.

I search through the wardrobe—*three times*—although it's quite obvious from even my first look inside that it isn't within.

When Georgie returns to my bedroom, to take me down for breakfast, she explains that my phone has been taken into 'super-vision' so that my 'abuser' won't be able to get into contact with me; or, presumably, so that *I* won't have the urge to get into contact with my abuser. Although the logic is sound, it really does little to help out my case here.

All I wanted was to get away . . . not to cut myself off from *everything*.

———

Looking about the breakfast room I see that it's a large hall with lofty, wooden beams soaring up overhead. Another ten or so women sit along the wooden benches, having their breakfast. Some sit alone, a few sit about in pairs; there's one trio.

Strong smells of buttery, scrambled eggs rise through the room. I breathe it all in, feel it tingle within my lungs. Already, I can feel my mouth beginning to water. It seems like an age since I last had something to eat.

I look to the breakfast buffet: three of those metal bowls covering their contents, one of those toasters with a feeder conveyor belt, and a large vat of coffee with one of those pouring spouts that has a lever. Although I'm sure the buffet will seem meagre in retrospect, like in about two hours, right now it appeals to me as just about the Most Delicious Thing *Ever*.

I grab one of the porcelain plates, take a couple of ready-toasted pieces of toast, smear on a healthy helping of butter, and then dish myself out some eggs on top.

I think long and hard about the tomato sauce, and decide that I should allow my figure this particular victory.

I do dose myself up with a healthy helping of black coffee, though.

At the end of the buffet, there's a pile of interlocking plastic trays.

I dump the contents of my breakfast on top.

After a brief period of looking like a lost lamb, wandering about the hall with my tray tight in my grasp, I find myself sitting beside the driver from the day before.

Today, rather than wearing the navy-blue jacket, she has on a waistcoat with shining brass buttons over a plain, white t-shirt. A pair of black jeans underneath. She also has the cap from the day before perched on her cropped, blond hair.

Her overall look is kinda rock 'n' roll.

"Hi," I say, taking a seat opposite her on the wooden bench.

She's tucking into her scrambled eggs, head bowed down to her porcelain plate. She glances up at me briefly, meets my eye for no longer than a second, gives me a nod of acknowledgement then returns to her eggs.

I glance about the hall, wondering if I've already made an irretrievable error in my sitting here, down by the driver. I haven't had time to figure out the politics of this place yet. To get my hands dirty with the who-sits-with-whos, and the don't-talk-to-thems.

"So," I say, forking up some eggs, "I have to go and see the *in-house* therapist later."

"Huh," the driver says—not a question, just an acknowledgement that she heard me and won't require me to repeat myself.

A subtle hint that I—*kindly*—button my lip.

I decide *not* to take the hint.

"I'm Anna," I say, "what's your name?"

The driver chews at her eggs, and I see that she's almost through with her breakfast. I wonder if she's picked up speed since I sat down here with her. She gives me another one of those fleeting glances. "Ursula," she says.

"Is that German?" I say.

The driver—*Ursula*—looks over and above my head.

When I turn to look, I can't see anybody there, and I suppose she was just doing her level best to avoid eye contact.

Just when I'm sure that she's forgotten about my question, she looks long and hard at me, then says, "I'm going to your house today—to pick up your things." She pauses for a moment to lick a stray fleck of ketchup from the corner of her mouth. "Anything in particular you don't want left behind?"

I give Ursula a steely glare.

I feel my stomach sink.

And I can't help thinking that I'm unnecessarily putting her into danger.

I have to tell her.

What's *really* going on.

———

For some reason, when I feed Ursula the truth, and nothing but, I expect her to flip out, to go and call up the tight security that's surely keeping a firm eye on this place.

Ursula gives a slight smile as she pops the last forkful of eggs and toast in through her lips. She shakes her head. "Now, I've heard some tall tales in my time," she says, "but now I've heard them all." She clucks her tongue, shakes her head again. "*Assassin*," she adds, in a sort of wondrous tone, as if she's genuinely impressed by my imaginative ingenuity.

As she heads off to deposit her tray at the window into the kitchen, I reach out and take hold of the hem of her waistcoat. She seems to take exception to this—well, she fires off a glare at where I hold onto her.

When I speak, my voice is weak, and—*I* think—almost impossible for Ursula to hear.

But I make sure she *does* hear.

"Listen," I say, "you don't have to believe all that I told you, but please, I *beg* you, when you go back to my house, you have to take care. Okay?"

Ursula meets my eye, and, in that moment, I detect a faint shift in her irises, that dark-brown colour of her eyes taking on a slightly purple tint. "Okay," she says, then looks back down to my hand, where I hold her.

I let go.

And Ursula deposits her tray at the kitchen window, then leaves the hall.

Chapter Twenty-Seven

AFTER BREAKFAST, I go back up to my bedroom, not having anybody else to tell me what I'm meant to do next. And since there's no sort of diversion in my bedroom, other than the bible in the drawer of the bedside table, I decide to take another shower.

Boredom is as boredom does . . .

Once showered and dressed—*again*—I find Georgie back outside my bedroom door.

That same smile on her lips.

And her puffed-out hair waiting for me.

She wears the same jumper from the day before, and her skin seems to have more of a youthful shine to it in the daytime. While last night I thought that she had to be over forty, now I'm not so sure that she's even past *twenty*.

"Take another shower?" Georgie says.

"Yeah," I say, not really thinking, "I spent a few days out in a field."

She purses her lips at this statement and I decide not to elaborate.

It's more *fun* this way.

"Ready to go see the therapist?" Georgie says, apparently forgetting the previous comment.

"Think so," I reply.

With that matter all cleaned up, the two of us trudge along the corridor.

I look down through the windows at the grounds of the building.

Golden sunlight beams down from the soggy-bottomed heavens.

When we pass by an open window, through which is drifting an absolutely *wicked* breeze, Georgie reaches out and draws it shut. As she turns back to me, she says, "This used to be a hospital."

"Really?" I say, not entirely unsurprised.

We continue on our way.

"Oh, it's been out of action for the best part of a century now, and the whole building was falling down all about the place before we moved in here."

"I see."

Georgie leads me on along the corridor, and then down a series of staircases.

We return to ground level and the décor of the corridors shifts from being simple, institutionally white-washed walls to wooden panels.

"This," Georgie explains as we walk along the corridor, "used to be where the surgeons would have their offices, where they would bring in patients—consult with them."

As I observe the doors, all of them open, I peer in on women sat at desks, typing away at computers, large filing cabinets filling most of the rooms. Some of the women smile and wave at Georgie—and me, *I suppose*—as we pass by.

We get close to the end of the corridor, when Georgie turns into me, and drops her voice to a conspiratorial whisper. "Don't try to hide anything," Georgie says, "that's the very worst thing you can do with Harriet."

" 'Harriet?' " I say, feeling that name tickle me a little.

It seems in keeping with the Victorian style of the building, in any case.

Georgie nods at me. "She's good—remember that she's seen all of us, at one time or another, when we arrived here. She knows how to help those in situations like us."

As Georgie steps back from me, knocks on the door, I wonder just what exactly 'Harriet' is going to make of me.

Nothing *good*, I imagine.

Not if I tell her the truth.

———

When I step into the office, I catch the damp, sweet smell of rotten banana. It catches in the back of my throat, doing combat with the scrambled eggs I got down only an hour or so ago. Like the other offices on this floor, it has a window looking out over the grounds, stretching into the distance. A little way beyond, I make out the gate to the grounds, and the white four-by-four which Ursula 'saved' me in the day before.

I bring my attention back to the foreground.

Take in the large—*too large?*—oak desk.

And the woman who sits at it, scratching away with a ball-point pen at some form or other. She has on a pair of silver-framed glasses, the lenses of which seem to have a pinkish tint to them. She looks to be well into her fifties—perhaps five or ten years into having those doughy, matronly characteristics catch up with her. She wears a silky, cream blouse with a purple neckerchief flourishing out from the collar.

I can't see her legs for the oak desk.

I glance back over my shoulder just in time to watch Georgie slip from the room, closing the door behind her as she goes out.

"Take a seat, please," the therapist—*Harriet*—says.

I do as I'm told.

The chair which stands before her mighty desk has one of those emerald-green cushions embedded in it. The type that, I'm sure, are popular in universities throughout the land.

And, apparently, in what used to be surgeons' offices.

I sit down on the cushion, immediately feeling as if all the air within the cushion seeps out from beneath my weight. Already I feel like I'm interrupting whatever important task Harriet's seeing to with those papers. I look to the bookshelves—a little sparse; just the odd hardback manual, here and there, all of them minus their dust jackets, and, as a consequence, *thick* with dust.

"Full name, please?"

Harriet's sharp voice catches me by surprise.

"Anna Harris," I reply, shortly.

Harriet nods to herself, scratches away at the paper.

I glance about the room again, only now realising that there's an ominous lack of a computer anywhere here. There's not even so much as a tablet computer that I can see. And neither is there any sort of sign of Harriet having personalised the room.

When Harriet finishes up with the form, she reaches up, then slides her glasses down her nose and rests them on the table. With her left hand, she massages the pockmarks left by the rubber supports of her glasses, and then, arching her shoulders back to get shot of an apparent ache, she blinks at me, cocks her head to one side, and says, "So, Anna, tell me how it happened."

For some reason I'm outraged, although I have no right at all to be . . . after all, this woman is supposed to be *sympathetic* to women in my position . . . women who are *thought* to be in my position.

What *is* my position, exactly?

I look long into Harriet's watery blue eyes, and I see scepticism there, as if she's looking through me. Like my skull isn't blocking her seeing into my brain.

Into my very thoughts.

When I don't answer her, Harriet lets loose a sigh, rises up from her seat, and strolls over to the bookshelf. I notice that she has a slight limp—her left leg. When she reaches the shelf, she slips off one of the enormous tomes I noticed from before. She blows across the surface, sending dust swilling through the air, ducking and diving, like waves breaking on a beach. Without another word to me, she lays the book flat on the desk, then peels it open to the first page. She uses her elbow as a crutch on the desk, resting her head on her palm. With her other hand, she reaches for her glasses, slips them back over the tip of her nose. Before she returns to scan the page lying spread out before her, she looks to me one more time, then says, "Any time you want to talk is quite all right by me, but I'm not about to sit here and allow you to waste my time."

It feels as if someone is *squeezing* my insides.

I square my shoulders, stare back at her.

"Why don't we cut the bullshit, huh?" I say to her, a little taken aback by my bile-tipped words.

Harriet raises her eyebrows. She sits up straight and lays both of her palms down flat across the pages of the opened book. "And what *bullshit* would that be, Anna?"

"You know," I say, looking past her now, out the window, out past the gate.

Almost trying to summon the white four-by-four back.

There's a long silence in the office, and it suddenly feels extremely frosty despite the large radiator, through which hot water gurgles.

I only realise I've been holding my breath when I feel as if my cheeks are about to burst.

I take a few little snorts of air through my nose.

Try to jig my heart back into its natural rhythm.

Turn my attention back onto Harriet.

"She talked to you, didn't she?" I say.

"Ursula?" Harriet says, with a thin smile . . . it's a pity that she doesn't use lipstick because it might be able to cure the bloodless quality of her lips. "Yes," she continues, "Ursula might've come into my office, told me what you said in the breakfast room."

"And?" I say. "Why all this . . . *therapy?* Why not just throw me out on my arse?"

Another silence, which Harriet finally breaks. "Because, Mrs Harris—"

"*Miss* Harris," I correct her.

She treats me to another one of her bloodless smiles. "Because, *Miss* Harris, the Winged Women's Institute is designed for women in need." She stops short for a long moment, and then adds, "And you, Anna, seem very much like a woman in need."

Chapter Twenty-Eight

THE MEETING WITH HARRIET goes on for another hour or so, wherein I do my very best to outline my situation. I don't worry about the ridiculousness of the thing, I tell myself that it's all *subtleties*, that if I can just find out what's happening to me . . . who these men are who're coming after me . . . then I can *fix* it all later on.

Harriet, like all good therapists, simply sits there, behind her desk, and listens patiently.

No interruptions.

And throughout the entirety of our conversation, her eyes don't *once* sneak downwards for a peek at the pages of the book spread out before her.

She agrees that I can stay, and I promise that, when all this is through, that I'll be giving the Winged Women's Institute an *extremely* generous donation. I have all intention of following through, although, quite frankly, I expect Harriet to reject my offer—accepting blood money in exchange for harbouring an assassin sounds like a bit of a stretch even for a cause as good as this one—but she surprises me, and says nothing.

Certainly, she doesn't *turn down* the money.

When I get through with the whole of my story, Harriet parts her lips, seems to search for expression for a couple of beats, before saying, "These men, you have absolutely no idea who they are? You're totally sure that you're telling me the truth about *that?*"

"Yes," I reply, without hesitation.

Harriet furrows her brow. She brings a clutched fist up to her lips, and then gazes around the office, back out the window, to the gate of the grounds. When I observe her face in profile, I see a smile crack her lips.

That's when I realise that she's *enjoying* this!

"It's just that, well," Harriet says, "this is probably me being silly, but what you said about the Chief Constable's daughter . . ."

"About Amy?"

"Yes," Harriet continues, "about *Amy*—don't you think that her father might well be looking for her?"

"That's what Brian told me."

Already I feel a sinking sensation in my gut, just to think about all the details I've spilled to this stranger I've just met. It's only then that I realise what Georgie said is true—that Harriet really is nothing short of an expert at what she does.

She can make people just *open* up.

"Those men," Harriet says, "couldn't it be that they're just searching for Amy, trying to bring her back home?"

I shake my head. "No, like I told you, Amy's father threw her out, he couldn't handle the fact that she wasn't his daughter . . . that was when she came to stay with me."

"Right," Harriet replies, "but don't you think that there might be some scope for him to have changed his mind?"

I breathe in the manky air, half-heartedly searching for that scent of rotten banana I first smelled when I set foot in the room. "I suppose so."

"And he came to you—looking for answers?"

"Yes," I reply.

Harriet interlocks her fingers, clenches her hands together, and then says, "What if you'd stuck around at home, if you'd just stayed to speak with those men?"

"You mean after they'd let themselves in the front door?"

Harriet nods in reply.

I find myself speechless, then I finally do find *some* words. "I . . . don't know . . . ."

With a smile, Harriet cocks her head to one side.

That purple neckerchief, I think, now, makes her look a little like a bird of paradise.

A wise one, perhaps.

But a bird of paradise *still*.

————

After the meeting, Harriet hands me back my mobile phone.

Fully charged.

I expect her to tell me to get out that second, but, instead, she gives me a stay of execution till the next morning, promising that Ursula can drive me back home.

When I finally leave Harriet behind in her office, when I'm finally alone out in the corridor, pacing back towards my bedroom, I can't help thinking that, in some way, I've acted as some sort of entertainment for Harriet . . . a little way for her to work at some real-life jigsaw puzzle. I suppose with the work she gets here, it must get grimly predictable.

She's seen it all, *heard* it all before.

She probably knew, the second that I rolled into the driveway of the Winged Women's Institute, that I wasn't for real.

For her it might only take a glance.

Back up in my bedroom, I flip my phone back on, check my messages.

There's one from Brian which reads, simply:

Be careful.
X

I give the message a little flash of my eyebrows, as if my mind alone might be able to transmit a response back to Brian.

Seeing there're no more messages from AA—beyond the one telling me that he's staying away from me to 'keep Amy safe'—I find myself at a bit of a loose end.

The weather's holding okay, so I grab a coat I find hanging up in the wardrobe, and head on out to have a walk about the grounds.

Just trudging about the fallow lawns does me good.

The winter's chill—just around the corner—nibbles at my ears.

At my cheeks.

At my fingertips.

In the course of my exploration, I come across a small bandstand: one of those cast-iron models, turned green from moss, its once pitch-black colour flaked away by years of use and weathering. Just standing there, leaning up against the frame, I can imagine what it must've been like to host parties here:

A *wedding*, perhaps.

I can almost hear the floating melodies of the strings, the marquees all spread out on the lawn, the people mulling about, back and forth, everybody with a flute of champagne in their hands. Children skittering about their feet.

Now, though, I don't imagine they host any parties at all.

Not parties like *that* anyway.

Parties that Brian Mathewson would be proud of.

"Anna?"

I turn to look, see that Georgie has rounded the building, and that she's approaching me.

Like me, she wears an overcoat, and she walks with her hands stuffed into her pockets, her breath coming out in clouds of steam. She feeds me a smile. "Harriet told me everything."

"She did?" I say.

Georgie nods. "I called up Ursula about twenty minutes ago, told her that she didn't need to cart your stuff all the way over here, but she'd already gone and done it." Georgie gives me a shrug coupled with a bug-eyed stare.

We stand there, looking out over the long grasses.

It's really quite beautiful, the wild flowers growing between the dark-green, long, flowing blades of grass. And I wonder why people cut their lawns at all.

Neighbourhood pressure, I guess . . .

"Are you angry?" I say, not wanting to turn back to meet Georgie's eye.

"No," she replies, "it's like Harriet told you, you're a woman in need, so it's our duty to help you."

I can't help but feel deeply touched by that statement, I know, for myself, if somebody had tried out such a deception on me—

and I'd *caught* them—then I never would've forgiven them, let alone *trusted* them again.

Georgie seems to get a touch fidgety. She presses her lips tightly together and then tries, three times, to tuck an unruly corkscrew curl behind her ear. Finally, she shifts closer to me, stands right at my ear, and whispers, "Is it true?"

"Is what true?"

"What Harriet said, what you told Ursula—about you being an assassin?"

I square my shoulders.

Look back at her.

I'm expecting to see fear.

To see her eyes swilling in their sockets, like a hare, ready to bolt at a second's notice, to get away from this aggressive, *unruly* person.

"Sure," I say, feeding Georgie a smile.

"Who do you kill?" Georgie says, actually coming closer to me.

I can feel the warmth of her breath up against my cheek now.

"Oh, whoever," I say, with a shrug.

Another long pause, then Georgie speaks up again. "And you never feel bad about it? I mean, you never find yourself thinking about it afterwards?"

I think about dishing it all out to Georgie, telling her about the therapist I used to have—*Julie*—and then think about informing her that I named my cat after one of my victims.

But instead, I just say, "No, not really."

Georgie just nods back at me as if she understands, and, I suppose, on some sort of surface level she *does* understand.

I mean, the job description of an assassin isn't rocket science.

———

Sure enough, Ursula crunches that white four-by-four in over the gravel driveway about fifteen minutes later. Although it's been less than a day since I was back home, it feels great to have my wardrobe back. I press my forehead up against the cool glass and peer in through the rear window of the four-by-four; look over the cardboard boxes all lined up in the back.

Three of them.

I thought I might have had more possessions than that.

Guess not . . .

When Ursula steps out of the driver's door, wearing the same waistcoat over the plain, white t-shirt from this morning at break-fast, she doffs her cap to me, rounds the car.

"Is this everything?" I say.

Ursula gives me something between a glare and a smirk as she reaches for the release handle to the boot. "Clothes, some makeup, a few pairs of shoes."

The boot opens up before us on its hydraulic arm.

That same, artificial odour of pine exhales from within.

Ursula turns back to me. "But," she says, "from what I've heard you won't be staying here much longer." Now her expression *is* definitely a smirk. "That's too bad."

I glance over the façade of the building—the façade of the ex-hospital—and I see Georgie standing there at the entrance, leaning on the stone wall, and looking out over the grounds, thinking of who-the-hell-knows what.

I call her over and, just like an obedient puppy, she bounces over to us, that same smile smeared all over her lips.

"Hey Ursula!" Georgie says.

Ursula gives a sort of grunt then treads her way back towards the entrance of the building. "When you're done sorting through the boot, just shut it behind you. It'll lock automatically in a minute or so after that."

And, with her parting comment, she disappears into the darkened interior of the entrance hall.

I turn to look at Georgie. "You think you could help me pick out an outfit for my Last Supper?"

Georgie beams back at me.

Although I was only half joking about the whole 'Last Supper' thing, Georgie puts all her efforts into selecting something appropriate for dinner that night. She picks through the cardboard boxes, and, I can't help noticing, that all my clothes are folded neatly.

Perhaps there's more than meets the eye with Ursula.

A tender core beneath that titanium exterior.

Finally, Georgie has me an outfit all picked out.

A scarlet cocktail dress.

Matching underwear.

I slip Georgie a sidelong glance and she gives me another one of those bright smiles, those smiles that, already, I feel like I'm going to miss once I'm turfed out of the grounds.

Right as we're about to slam the boot shut again, allow the car to automatically click on its locking system, Georgie barks out, "Got a *scarf?*"

"A scarf?" I say, thinking of a thick, woollen thing.

"Yes," she says, "you know, just a thin one, like a pashmina?"

I turn my attention back to the cardboard boxes, nodding to myself. "Actually," I say, "I think there is one around here some-place, let's take a look."

As I dig through the cardboard box, searching for the pash-mina, I hear a high-pitched squeal emanate from Georgie.

Operating on instinct, I spin around, glance about me.

Back to the gate of the grounds, thinking that she's seen something there.

Not seeing anything in particular, except for the rusted-up, old gate; I turn my attention back to the foreground. To the boot.

Georgie's taken several steps back from the cardboard box.

I give a slight smile. "What is it?" I say. "A spider? My cat's left a 'present' in there, has she?"

Georgie can't speak—it seems as if her lips have become frozen shut.

"What?" I say, frowning, and then approach the box which Georgie has been digging through, searching for the pashmina.

"I found it," Georgie finally gets out, her voice lacking power, any sort of substance really, "the pashmina."

I look down into the cardboard box and, indeed, see the pashmina there.

And the reason for Georgie's reaction.

The pashmina half conceals a gun.

One which I haven't seen in my entire life.

———

I stare for a long time at the gun, trying to take it in.

It's a serious piece of kit: a 9mm service pistol; clip already in place.

I glance back at Georgie, a frown sketched on my brow. "I don't know where this has come from," I say.

Georgie's eyes are wide, as if there's a snake coiled in this cardboard box. She backs away another few steps.

I turn back to the open cardboard box, reach down and inspect the gun.

The safety's switched off.

When I try to snap it on, it's jammed.

It needs lubricant.

Just from looking over the exterior casing, I can see that it hasn't been treated particularly well. That it's—most likely— been shoved into a sock drawer for years, if not decades. Some- body who doesn't know the first thing about guns has had hold of it.

I turn back to Georgie, shake my head. "It's not mine."

Georgie remains struck dumb.

When I glance up, I notice Ursula leaning up against one of the stone pillars of the entrance hall, smoking a cigarette. Before I proceed, I look back to Georgie, then snatch up the pashmina, quickly wrap the gun up inside; conceal it beneath my cocktail dress which I drape over my arm.

I note Georgie staring long and hard at me, and I do my best to reassure her. "Believe me, this is safest with me, okay?"

Georgie stares at my cocktail dress, as if she has X-ray vision, and can see nothing but the gun which I conceal.

"Come on," I say, with a smile to Georgie.

This seems to lighten her up a little.

"Remember to shut the boot," I say, stepping away from the car.

When we reach the entrance to the building, I turn straight to Ursula, blowing out a steady stream of smoke into the frosty air. "You did a good job in folding my clothes, in sorting them into the cardboard boxes." My throat constricts a little as I await her reaction, but I manage to get out a strained, "Thanks."

Ursula sucks in another lungful of smoke, blows it out again.

She drops her finished cigarette butt on the ground, crushes it with her heel.

Then she squares her shoulders, makes for the entrance of the building. "Don't mention it," she says, "your neighbour was the one who got all your clothes in order. I just showed up and all the boxes were already packed." She shudders a little from the cold. "Easy."

Chapter Twenty-Nine

I FINALLY SHAKE OFF GEORGIE, who seems to have got over her initial shock at seeing the gun. I send her off in the direction of the bathroom, while I mutter something about her needing to take a shower, to get ready for tonight.

That done, and finally alone in my bedroom, with night falling outside, I lay the gun down carefully on my bedside table, just stare at it for a long few moments. I try to square just what's gone on here. Of course, I recall what Mrs Pietersen said about having a gun . . . that *this* must be the gun that she was alluding to. And yet, at the same time, I can't quite figure out why she's thought to give it to me. She claimed that she was sending me somewhere safe . . . and, anyway, just how does she get off handing me something which can kill?

Once I'm done with my pondering, I realise that time is of the essence.

I slip out of my bedroom, happen across a maintenance cupboard.

There's nothing really suitable, so I have to settle for a spray can of household lubricant.

Back in my bedroom, I set about, first, trying to loosen up the safety catch. After a couple of hearty sprays, I can get just enough purchase to slip it into place.

Next, I turn my attention to the clip, squeezing it out, and seeing that it's nearly full.

Although I'm not about to check, I suppose that there's a bullet already in the chamber, ready to be fired.

I slide open the drawer of my bedside table, lay the gun down inside, then look over my frock for the evening.

For the life of me, I can't recall having ever bought it—let alone having *worn* it.

But it wouldn't be here if it wasn't so, unless Mrs Pietersen, the wily old minx, decided to sneak this smoky little number inside that cardboard box of tricks.

When Georgie returns to my bedroom, wrapped in a towel, I'm already wearing the dress. Georgie stands still in the doorway, her mouth latched open, apparently unable to believe what I'm wearing. I hope that it's the *good* kind of surprise.

"How does it look?" I say.

Georgie gives a slight shake of her head, as if lost for words.

That makes me feel better.

There's nothing so pleasant as having your confidence boosted.

The two of us, not unlike giddy school girls, traipse along the hallway, down towards Georgie's bedroom. In Georgie's bedroom, I latch open her own steel wardrobe, see that she, really, has quite a nice choice within.

"Where'd you get the threads?" I say.

"Oh," Georgie replies, "here and there." She can't hold back any longer, and she bursts into an all-out smile. "I tend to be the first one to go rummaging through the donations when they come in."

For some reason, I feel something catch in my throat.

As I sit on the edge of my bed in my scarlet little number, the pashmina draped about my neck, with my legs crossed—like an *elegant* girl—I observe Georgie pull out one dress after another. Each of the dresses is encased in protective black plastic. I can tell that either Georgie sends these dresses out to be dry cleaned straight after wearing each one, or she hasn't had much of an occasion to wear them.

Until now.

In the end, we go for an emerald-green dress, one with straps about the neck, and a slightly ruffled hem. Feeling like I'm about sixteen years old, I lead Georgie down the corridor, back to the bathroom, and to the full-length mirror. I stand at Georgie's shoulder as she peers at her reflection.

I'm not quite sure what sets it off, perhaps it's seeing herself in a dress again, but I notice the sparkle of tears in Georgie's eyes. Before I know it, she holds her hands up to her mouth and nose, sobbing away.

Silently.

I round her, take hold of her shoulders, firmly. "Georgie?" I say. "Georgie? What's the matter? Do you want me to go and fetch Harriet?" I pause for a moment, look over Georgie's shoulder, to the door of the bathroom.

See Ursula standing there.

Just staring at us.

That waistcoat of hers hanging baggy over her stocky frame.

"What?" I say. "What'd you want?"

Ursula wrinkles her nose. "What's all this about?"

"I don't know," I say. "I thought that we'd dress up."

"*Why?*" Ursula says, her tone fraught, *mean*.

"For fun," I say, turning back to Georgie, and her eerily silent tears. I slip a hand down her side, to her own hand dangling there. I interlock her fingers with my own. "Come on," I say to Georgie, "it's all okay, you can tell me what the matter is."

"Good luck," Ursula says, with a shake of her head as she departs. "She never tells anybody anything. Not even Harriet."

I scowl long and hard at Ursula as she slips from the bathroom, fantasising what sorts of things I might do to get even.

I've never really been able to tolerate bullies.

I spend another few minutes shushing Georgie into a state where she can speak again. When she will meet my eyes with her own tear-soaked ones. I give her hand a squeeze. "You're safe," I say, "she's gone now—*Ursula's* gone now."

Georgie slips her hand out of mine. She balls her fingers into a pair of fists then rubs at her eyes, almost like a toddler, or what seems to *me* like a toddler.

"What is it?" I say, crouching down to her, it seeming like the thing to do. "What's the matter with the dress?"

Georgie's mouth breaks out into a smile, and I see a youthful, positive glimmer in her eye—a silver lining. "No," she says, "it's not *the dress*, it's just that . . . that . . . it makes me think of . . . of . . . *him*."

"What about him?" I say, reaching for her now-unoccupied hand, taking hold of it.

Giving it another squeeze.

Georgie shakes her head, already claiming that she can't find the strength to reply.

But I meet her eye, force her gaze onto mine.

"Hey?" I say. "Didn't you see that gun which cropped up in

the cardboard box, out there in the car? Do you really think I'm about to let anybody hurt you? Look on the bright-side, you've got a trained assassin here with you."

Georgie looks to me with those large, round eyes of hers. Finally she seems to catch hold of herself, to be able to stop the silent tears from spilling from her eyes. "I never"—*sniff, sniff*—"thought that he'd . . . he'd"—*sniff, sniff*—"he was never that sort of . . . of"—*sniff, sniff*—"person."

I clench Georgie's hand a little tighter.

She takes a couple of shuddering breaths.

I turn my attention down to her hand, to the gold-banded diamond clinging to her ring finger. I look back into her eyes and she sees that *I've* seen. "Is that from him?" I say.

Georgie presses her lips tightly together, pressing all the blood out of them.

She nods.

"You know what you should do with that ring?" I say.

She shakes her head.

"Throw it away."

Georgie's eyes become even wider—even *rounder*—if that's at all possible.

Although she probably doesn't take any steps back from me, it feels as if she retreats from me somehow, as if the force of memory tugs at her sleeve, urging her to return.

To *go back*.

"The thing about the past," I continue, staring at the ring now, "is that we have to learn to let it go." I lock my eyes back onto hers.

There's not even a glimmer of Georgie's familiar, apparently *carefree* smile that she's worn for the duration of my stay here. And I make it something of a mission to bring it back.

As soon as possible.

With a slight smile of my own, I jerk my head in the direction of one of the toilet cubicles. "Over there," I say, "toss it into the toilet bowl." When I speak again, I'm a touch surprised by the *snarling* tone in my voice. "*Flush it,*" I say.

I release her hands.

Stand up.

Give her some space.

Georgie stares at me for the longest time. Her other hand goes instinctively to the ring finger, she twists at the ring as if it was searing hot, as if she would like nothing more than to yank it off, but it's already brandished too far down into her skin.

I know that there's nothing I can do to help beyond what I've already said.

I can only watch.

And wait.

Several times, I believe that Georgie's going to bolt from the bathroom, that she's going to turn her back on me, run off . . . have me cast out of the grounds before time.

Before tomorrow morning.

And then, without any external reaction—*decision*—I can possibly observe, Georgie heads towards one of those toilet cubicles: the one closest to the window looking out over the grounds.

I feel my heart flutter up to my throat. A layer of sweat breaks out over the surface of my skin. Sends a chill passing through me. I give a shudder. Feel as if something—*Magic? Electricity?*—crackles through the air.

I realise that this is something which has bubbled beneath the surface for perhaps years. Ever since Georgie has arrived here, to the Winged Women's Institute.

Nearby, I hear the almost indiscernible *splish!*

Although it's such a tiny sound, it seems to echo about the bathroom.

To keep coming back to me.

I hold myself still, feel my heart beating against my ribcage.

Another step.

Another one to go.

And, right as I hear a bell reverberating throughout the corridors of the building—somebody calling the women to dinner?—I hear the unmistakable swill and *swish* of the toilet flushing.

Chapter Thirty

G RANTED, ME AND GEORGIE are something of an odd pair down at dinner, in the hall.

The other women, almost invariably dressed in jeans and baggy t-shirts, and jumpers; tuck into their mashed potatoes and sausages, sat on the wooden benches.

Me and Georgie giggle between ourselves, making puddles of gravy on our plates.

It's all I can do to stop myself turning my attention to Georgie's now-vacant ring finger, and seeing that there's nothing there any longer. Nothing else except for an indentured, red mark. When I glance along the wooden bench, I see Ursula sitting right on the end.

She has nobody sitting opposite, or beside her.

It's almost as if there's some unspoken rule—or perhaps with Ursula it *is* spoken—that there's a one-seat, no-go zone surrounding her.

As I meet Georgie's eye across the table, it appears that we have the same idea at the same time.

The two of us grab up our plastic trays; what remains of our bangers and mash swilling about in the gravy on the surface of each of our plates.

I take a seat on the bench beside Ursula, while Georgie takes her place opposite.

Ursula glances up from her plastic tray, eyes each of us, then says, "What're you two so happy about?" Without either me or Georgie saying a word, her eyes drift downwards, on instinct, to Georgie's hands. To her fingers. She looks up again. "Your ring?" she says, a slight smirk on her lips. "You finally tossed it away?"

I prepare myself to be a shoulder to cry on, but, against what I anticipate, Georgie just beams all over the place. Apparently still riding the high of having flushed that ring down the toilet. Perhaps the tears will come later.

Once dinner is over with, and, having eaten their way through the rice-pudding dessert, some of the women get to their feet.

Never having been the loudest voice in the room, but not seeing any other way to deal with the situation, I thrust myself up off the wooden bench, clear my throat, and give it all the wellie I've got. *"Dancing!"* I shout out, feeling my throat reverberate with the effort.

A touch of pain there too.

All the women, on the way out of the hall, pause to look over at me.

But, then again, why *wouldn't* they?

I am standing in the middle of the place barking out like a mad woman.

There's a case of nervous muttering passing among the room,

and, when I look over to the other side of the place, I see that Harriet is there.

Getting to her feet.

I feel my heart strike my ribs, and I catch a chilly sensation through my blood, like that reaction I would get back at school, feeling that I might be in line for a telling-off.

I see that, like earlier today, Harriet wears a cream blouse with that same purple neckerchief. I ready myself for a dressing down.

But, with a slight smile, Harriet meets my eye, looks off across the crowd, and then gives a nod to someone.

From out of nowhere, the sound of a cheesy eighties track plays—which one, I'm really not sure. Harriet claps her hands together, motions to the other women to help her in lugging the wooden benches out of the way.

I slip Georgie a sidelong glance, and we're close enough so that I can make my voice heard over the music. "Is this normal?" I say.

Georgie gives me a shake of the head, her lips slightly parted.

When I look over to Harriet, I catch her eye another time, and she gives me a wink in return. I can't help but feel a warmth rising in my gut—a feeling of *belonging* not just here, but *somewhere* for the first time in a long time. Harriet—*these women here*—they know just who I am . . . just *what* I am; and they couldn't care less.

I look around the hall, and see the women drifting back, most of them as surprised as Georgie is. None of them head back out, to go off to bed.

Well, *one* of them does.

I look up to see Ursula dropping her plastic tray with a neat *slap* on top of the pile, on the wooden buffet table. The sound of the dropping tray, somehow, cuts through the low throbbing bass of the current song.

Ursula slips from the hall without another word to anyone; and without anyone seeming to notice.

I'm half thinking about going to fetch her, when Georgie grabs me by the crook of my elbow, and guides me on towards the *impromptu* dance floor.

And I think that life's too short to try and cater for every hangdog.

———

I don't think I can recall having danced for so long since I gave up drinking.

When I glance at the screen of my mobile, I see that it's well past midnight. Although a few of the women have slipped off to bed, there's still a healthy crowd gathered in the hall, partying the night away. It's only when I look to Georgie, her emerald-green dress a little ruffled from all the dancing, that I catch Harriet's eye over her shoulder.

Harriet's *glower*.

Our eyes remain glued together for another few beats of my heart, before one of the women draws Harriet's attention away from me.

And I know that those feelings of acceptance were only fleeting, that I'm no more welcome here for who I am—*what I am*—than anywhere else in the world.

I know when it's time to exit a party.

I reach out for Georgie's shoulder, give it a slight squeeze, and she looks to me, her mouth still torn wide with her smile. I smile back at her, and then gesture towards the exit of the hall. She catches my meaning and the two of us head off that way.

Away from the droning, unstoppable music.

Off out to the cool air of the corridor.

We walk together, heading through the deserted building—the building which feels like a shoe several sizes too large for its foot, even during the day, with women up and about, out of bed; not dancing.

When we get back up to the floor we share, I turn to Georgie, expecting to give her a quick hug goodnight, but, instead, she pushes me hard up against the wall.

Presses her lips up against mine.

In the half-light of the corridor, my eyes remain very much open, and I'm very aware of staring at the backs of her closed eyelids. Before the kiss goes much further, Georgie pulls away from me, still grinning from ear to ear. She gives an apologetic little shrug of her shoulders. "Sorry," she says, "got carried away, I guess."

"Yeah," I say, giving her a smile back.

"It's a shame you have to go," Georgie says, "it's been fun to have you around—even if it was just for a very short time."

I feel my heart sink in my chest, but then I remind myself of that scowl on Harriet's face, and I know that I've worn out whatever welcome I had here.

And it's not like I'm interested in 'experimenting' either.

Girls just don't do it for me.

Never have—never will.

Probably . . .

As I stand there, watching Georgie's emerald-green dress twitch away into the gloom of the corridor, I slip out my mobile.

No messages.

Nobody loves me, or so it seems.

I pace on towards my bedroom, pause at the door, feeling that something's off . . . but I shrug it away. I reach out for my doorknob. Twist it. Feel the *clickety-click* of the hidden mechanism. As I push it forwards, I get another one of those shivers down my spine.

I stare into the darkness.

"Who's there?" I say, reaching for my mobile phone.

Bringing it up in my hand.

Shining the bluish-white backlight over the scene.

Nothing.

Just a ghostly-pale impression of my bedroom.

I breathe in, sure that I can smell deodorant on the air.

I tread all the way up to the window, peer through it, down onto the grounds below. To the cars parked up there.

Nothing out of the ordinary.

I give a shake of my head, at my stupidity, and then I turn around, into the darkness; still unable to completely lose the sense that there *is* someone here.

Or that there *was* someone here.

With my eyes still very much fixed onto the gloom, I go about undressing, slipping off my dress, my high heels. I rub at the marks on my ankles from the straps. Flex my toes out, feeling my muscles cracking from all the years of running . . . I hope that cardio work was better for my heart than it was for my joints . . .

I help myself into bed, putting on the same pyjamas I wore the night before, and then, just because I can't get it off my mind, I get up, go over to the wardrobe, open it up, peer inside. Again, there's nothing there at all.

Nothing but stainless steel and vacant coat hangers.

I return to bed, now feeling *thoroughly* fed-up with myself.

It's only when I'm on the very cusp of sleep that I think of another thing.

One last thing to check.

I sit up straight, grab for the bedside-table drawer.

Pad about inside.

Looking for the gun.

It's gone.

Chapter Thirty-One

I WISH I COULD SAY that this is the first time I've 'misplaced' a firearm of mine.

But that would be a lie.

I'm up and out of bed, frantically looking in all the places where I might've left it . . . but there's nothing at all to find.

It's quite simple—it's *lost*.

With not a little dramatic flair, my bedroom door creaks open.

A form is silhouetted by the dim glow of the hallway lights.

"Can't find it, can you, Anna?"

I hear the throaty voice, emanating from the silhouetted figure.

Heat rushes up to my cheeks.

"Couldn't leave it behind, could you?"

My eyes adjust.

I pick out the features from the shadows.

My brain puts together the pieces.

Ursula.

Now she wears a long trench coat, I realise, and that she has the collar turned up.

Perhaps that was the reason why I failed to recognise her right away.

I couldn't see the shape of the waistcoat she was wearing this evening.

But she still has on the cap from before.

That should have been enough—*would have been enough* . . . under normal circumstances.

Although I'm slightly ashamed to admit it, there's no way around it.

I let my guard down.

Allowed myself to relax for just one second, and this is what happens.

Ursula stands in the doorway with both her hands stuffed into her pockets. I can just about make out the slight smirk on her face.

My assassin's brain tries to judge whether or not she carries the gun in her pocket, if she has it pointed at me, ready to squeeze the trigger and leave a bloody Anna-Harris-shaped stain against the wall.

Ursula shakes her head. "This place, it's supposed to be a refuge, somewhere these women can be safe from the outside world—from the *violent* outside world." She stares at me long and hard from the doorway. "And you've ruined it—you've *taken advantage* of it."

It's only then that I feel the penny drop, and I can't stop myself from blabbing my mouth. "You're in love with Georgie, aren't you?" I say.

There's a long period of silence, and then Ursula says, "

'Love' is such a namby-pamby term, don't you think? What's wrong with *want?*"

I hold off for several beats and then say, "You're going to kill me then? Will that make it even?"

I feel my chest tighten as Ursula shifts her hands in her pockets, lifts them out.

I expect to see the shape of the gun there, to see it being pointed at me.

But, when she does remove her hands, holds them down at her sides, there's nothing.

"What do you take me for, Anna?" Ursula says. "Do you really think that I'd drop down to your level? That I'd decide to kill people for money? Although I imagine that would make an attractive headline for your boss, for Brian Mathewson, wouldn't it, now?"

I flinch just from hearing Brian's name, and it's too late, the reaction too *involuntary*, for me to do anything at all about it.

"What drives a person to do what you do, Anna? What makes you think that taking away people's lives is in *any way* an honest trade?"

To tell the truth, I have no response to her other than, 'I'm good at it,' but I don't come out with that, don't even utter it under my breath.

Instead, I say, "Guess I never had the opportunity to do anything so noble as saving helpless maidens."

Another long pause, then Ursula's smile widens. She breathes in deeply, her shoulders arching back. "Maybe that's it, maybe it's all about circumstance—perhaps, if I'd only chosen other opportunities along the road, if I'd only taken another direction, we wouldn't have turned out so differently, hmm?"

I feel like I want to prod at Ursula's own past, like jabbing my fingers into an open wound—*twisting*.

But I hold myself off.

For some reason, seeking the moral high ground.

Ursula breathes out long and hard—a truly *satisfied* sigh. "Sleep well, won't you, Anna? I hope not having your *weapon* to hand won't impinge on your quality of sleep."

With that, she turns her back to me.

Something within my killer's brain tells me to strike.

And I know, if I only chose to flip my Kill Switch, it would all go away.

But I don't.

Now's not the time.

As she slips from view, out of the doorway, and down the corridor, she mutters, "Nighty night."

Chapter Thirty-Two

MAYBE URSULA read me better than I thought, because, for long—*strung-out*—periods of the night, I toss and turn, unable to find any sleep. When I feel the golden dawn light sweeping in through the letterbox window above, I shuck my blankets and set about getting myself dressed.

Ready for my Big Exit.

Today, sensing that it's going to be a day of blazing blue, autumn skies, I slip on a light-yellow tank top beneath a woolly jumper. I prod my feet into the ankle-high boots I've been wearing for what seems like a decade.

Then I fold my dress up, tuck it under my arm, and go down to breakfast.

When I leave the bedroom behind for the last time—leave my temporary refuge behind—I don't even bother to look back.

I get through with breakfast as quickly as I can manage, vaguely aware of the cardboard-texture of the cereal, hardly tasting the fresh milk which, Georgie dizzily tells me, is produced just down the road.

I meet Ursula's eye, across the hall, and, without a word to her, I head off to the entrance hall of the building and wait for her.

While I lean up against the stone archway of the entrance, with Georgie standing beside me, jabbering away about everything and anything, Harriet emerges to give me an extremely formal—not to mention *cold*—handshake, before turning back into the building.

As I stare at her retreating heels, I can't help but feel the burn of resentment still cling to the air.

She simply can't stand me.

I imagine the scene, having sent her a cheque, the brown envelope appearing on the desk before her, and then, seeing the name, Harriet tearing it into tiny strips, bundling those strips into a tight ball, before promptly tossing them into the wicker bin in the corner of her sizeable office.

On the other hand, a direct debit might be a better option . .
.

Ursula, that cap of hers resting on her brow, and today wearing that more formal, navy-blue jacket—the same one she had on when she first picked me up—doesn't so much as look at me. She simply squeezes the plastic fob, sending the amber hazard lights of the white four-by-four blinking.

Pulls open the driver's door.

Gets in.

She starts the engine.

Revs it a couple of times.

Impatient.

I turn to Georgie, whose ever-present smile has now slipped off her face. I can see that her eyes are beginning to water. Before I can think of anything consoling to say to her, she throws her arms about my neck, and tugs me down into the bulky, fluffy, zip-up fleece she wears; the one which conceals her sleek figure.

"Thank you," I hear her gasp into my ear, and then, as she pulls away from me, as I feel the tears soaking into my shoulder, "And sorry . . ."

We stare at one another for a good few moments, and I feel a twisting sensation in the pit of my gut, that twisting-knife sensation of leaving someone I care very much about.

And we hardly know one another.

She interlocks her fingers with mine, squeezes and then, with a departing smile, a tear snaking its way down her cheek, she mouths a goodbye.

Not wanting to elongate this moment any more than necessary, I turn my back to her.

Get into the passenger seat of the car.

With Ursula.

————

The strong, artificial smell of pine rips through the air of the car, and it's all I can do to stop it from overwhelming me, from sending nausea rippling through my blood. When I glance up to the rear-view mirror, I see that Georgie has gone . . . that she no longer stands outside the entrance.

And I think it's better.

Better this way.

Goodbyes are painful enough.

The engine idles and I look to Ursula, waiting to see what's going to happen next.

I can see, in the rear-view mirror that all the boxes of my possessions—of the ones Mrs Pietersen 'rescued' for me—are still stowed in the boot.

Ursula simply sits in the driver's seat, her leather-gloved hands on the wheel, gripping tightly. "Open the glove compartment," she says.

I give her a scowl, then do what she tells me.

Within, illuminated by the dim, orange light, I see the gun.

I slip Ursula a sidelong glance.

She continues to look out through the windscreen, at some invisible spot in the middle distance. "Don't trust myself with it," she says.

I feel a tingle passing through me as I reach out for the gun.

I see that it's how I left it: safety switched on.

Everything looking in good shape.

Not having anywhere obvious to stow the gun, and not able to stash it in the waistband of my jeans because of comfort issues, I lay it down on my lap.

Ursula revs the engine once more, and then pulls out, sending gravel pinging against the underside of the car.

———

We've been driving for about five minutes before I realise that we're being followed.

I can see them in the wing mirror, on my side of the car.

An estate car—*inconspicuous*—similar in size and style to Mark's.

I feel the blood well up to my temples.

I glance across at Ursula, and, although she looks back at me, there's no need for words.

That smirk on her lips says it all.

It says that when she returned to my house, she struck a deal with those men; let them know precisely where I was. And then she made them promise to be patient, to bide their time, parked outside of the Winged Women's Institute.

To await their signal.

I'm on the brink of reaching out, making a grab for the steering wheel to haul us off the narrow country lane, off onto the grassy verges, taking a chance that the car doesn't flip into a ditch, when I turn my attention back downwards.

To the gun there.

In my lap.

And I realise that Ursula could've kept it to herself.

She could've left me high and dry.

But she's given me the means to defend myself.

Ursula drives on. When she speaks, she doesn't so much as look at me once.

I would think that she's concentrating on the road ahead, if I didn't know that the road is as straight as one of those corridors back at the Winged Women's Institute.

"In about quarter of a mile there's a humpback bridge—a thick forest to the left of it. I'll drop you off on the other side. If you follow the stream, you'll get to a motorway service station, about fifteen minutes' walk—if you're quick."

Despite the situation, despite having these goons back following me; I manage to raise a smile. "Sounds like you've done this before."

She smiles back at me, in profile. "Here it comes," she says.

Chapter Thirty-Three

I HIT THE GROUND HARD.

Rocks sting my palms.

My kneecaps hit the earth.

I roll onto my side, into the damp grass.

For a few seconds, I lie on my back.

My breath forms clouds before my eyes.

The air bites my cheeks.

The engine of the four-by-four roars away.

Replaced by the sound of the pursuing car.

The estate with the men.

Get up, Anna.

GET UP!

I breathe in the sweet smell of the grass, can smell pine—*real pine*—from the trees which now surround me.

I roll my hips.

Stumble to my feet.

Look to my left.

Just like Ursula told me.

I see the pine trees.

Their shapes like stiff-bristled brushes.

The engine of the car behind grows louder.

I hear it hit a high gear.

The *crunch!* of tyres skidding to a halt on the country lane.

Shouting.

I put one foot in front of the other.

Almost take a tumble.

But hold myself upright.

I sink my teeth into my lower lip.

It brings my mind sharp.

Brings my concentration back with a *snap*.

I remember.

Look down.

See the gun, lying there.

In the grass.

At my feet.

I stoop for it.

Gather it.

Grip hold.

Then I break into a run.

I build up speed.

One foot after the other.

My ankle-high boots weigh me down.

Threaten to haul me over.

Easy does it.

I dial back into what Ursula said.

Spot the stream.

Down at my feet.

I see the water gurgle along.

Shimmy through the rocks.

A *shallow* stream.

The water smells clean.

Pure.

It urges me onwards.

Into the trees.

The engine switches off.

Only the sound of footfalls.

And of shouting voices.

One man communicating with the other.

My heart beats against my tonsils.

Sweat forms at the base of my spine.

Perhaps the woolly jumper wasn't the *best* fashion choice.

I slip on a loose rock.

Catch myself on a rugged tree trunk.

With my free hand.

Hold myself up.

Stop myself from taking a tumble.

The gun slips a little in my grasp.

I get a better hold on it.

The men still shout.

Their footfall sounds closer still now.

I urge myself on.

Fifteen minutes' walk.

To the service station.

A five-minute run?

Guess I'm going to see.

I take long paces.

Never stopping to look over my shoulder.

I bow my head.

Miss low-hanging branches.

I dodge between tree trunks.

My teeth sink deeper into my lip.

I taste blood in my mouth.

All around my mouth.

I trip over a trailing root.

I feel myself falling.

And almost . . . *almost* . . . catch myself.

Stop myself going down.

But it's then when something—*something*—snaps inside me.

And I just give up.

Just for a moment.

A moment's all it takes.

Down, down, down.

Through the air.

And *hard* onto the soft soil.

Lined with pine needles.

They jab into my cheeks.

Into my palms.

I breathe in.

Try to breathe out.

Something feels *wrong* . . . in my chest . . . *something's wrong.*

The bootfalls surround me on all sides.

Hunters cornering their prey.

Preparing for the *coup de grâce*.

Just one shot.

All it takes.

To stop this killer.

I wait for it to come.

Chapter Thirty-Four

I EXPECT THE *CRACK!* of a gunshot.

This would be the perfect place.

But it never comes.

Instead, I feel the arms, all around me, taking *hold* of me, and leading me off through the pine trees, back in the direction I came. As they grab hold of me, I glance to my side. I see the stream there, burbling along, its water continuing to flow downstream, to the petrol station, to the destination I will never reach.

In my daze, in this forced march, I feel a lingering question on my lips. Perhaps I hit my head, or maybe it's the pain in my chest. Where I must've struck a root.

Or a rock.

"The gun . . . the gun?" I say, one half a question; the other a statement.

A voice answers me; a thick, Scottish accent.

Glasgow?

"Don't you worry, lassie, we got it just fine."

I allow my head to bob down on my chest.

I can feel my brain ebbing away from me now.

Sleep beckoning me inside.

I blink several times.

Bite my lip hard.

But it's no use.

I can't stay afloat.

Because I know . . . back there . . . that I gave up.

———————

I come around to the sound of a mobile phone vibrating.

It pricks my ears like a mosquito.

There's a thrumming in my ears.

Almost like I've been sat on a plane for hours and hours.

My brain lost to the drawling, insurmountable engine noise.

Feeling as if cotton wool sits just below the surface of my skin.

I crook open an eye.

The bluish-white glare from the phone illuminates the boxy, windowless room.

I see I'm lying on a mattress.

One of those camp-bed mattresses.

A *fold-up* job.

Thin.

Just about feasible for a decent night's sleep.

I ease myself up onto an elbow.

Glance about me.

Recall the phone buzzing away.

I crawl over to where the phone lies, on the floor. When my palms make contact with the floor, I feel that it's concrete. A chill passes through my blood. Pain too. As I reach out for the phone, an uncontrollable pain wracks my chest. I almost double over. But I force myself onwards. To take hold of the phone.

To accept the call.

But, when I glance at the screen, I see that it's not a caller at all.

It's the low-battery notification.

When I glance over the screen, I see that the tiniest sliver of battery remains.

And then, as simply as flipping a switch, the screen goes dark.

The phone *dies* in my palm.

Darkness reigns once more.

I suck in air.

It feels stilted—*recycled*.

I wonder where I am.

I think back to the woods, to all those arms holding me. To how they held me tight, not allowing me so much as an inch to move. And I remember asking about my gun.

The Glaswegian accent.

Telling me that *they* had it.

Trying not to move too much—it seems the only way to avoid pain—I ease myself around, and rest my back up against the wall of the room. I feel the cool concrete through my woolly jumper.

It brings my senses alive.

Allows me to better see into the pitch-black room.

Outside, I can hear voices.

Drifting along the corridor.

I tune them in.

Try to make *sense* of them.

I can hear *gruff* male tones.

No surprise there.

Because it's *always*—one way or another—men.

I try to recall the little I was able to take in of the room while my mobile-phone screen still offered me light. Before it conked out of battery.

Just the flimsy mattress.

And concrete walls.

Nothing more.

I hear footsteps approaching.

Or they *seem* to be approaching.

I turn my head to look at the door.

I roll my shoulders; try to make my muscles supple.

There might be a fight coming.

I have no idea what happened to me out in the woods, that tiny moment when I *know* I could've caught my balance . . . but *didn't.*

A hefty key sounds in a lock.

There's the *clink-clank* of an aged locking mechanism.

Light floods the room all of a sudden.

I hold up my forearm.

Block my retinas from the glare.

A silhouette—*so much like Ursula*—stands there.

In the doorway.

"Comfy, Anna?"

It's Amy.

Chapter Thirty-Five

S OMEONE—*SOMEWHERE*—FLIPS A SWITCH.
Fluorescent lights blink on overhead.

This glare isn't as bright as the corridor lights.

But it causes me pain just the same.

As if it's another layer of torture.

I tune into the low-level *buzz* of the lights.

Feel like I can smell burning in the air.

I look to Amy, am vaguely conscious of her stepping into the room. That smell of strawberry-scented perfume wafts on in with her. She gives that wiggle of her nose; the one which, I'm sure, her beaux believe make her look like a cute, little bunny rabbit.

If *only* they knew.

The backstabbing *bitch.*

Her sapphire-blue eyes scope out the room, as if judging me purely based on where I've happened to wake up. On where these men have—*apparently*—brought me.

She bunches her shoulders up, and looks over at me.

She's wearing a beige overcoat, and, like Ursula, she holds her hands stuffed into her pockets. I can't help wishing she was Ursula right now.

That she had the steady moral compass of Ursula.

Amy wears the collar of the overcoat turned up, apparently to hide the scar at her throat . . . no amount of plastic surgery will be able to make the bite from the dog go completely away.

"Having fun?" Amy asks, a slight look of amusement in her eyes.

I can't even think about how to comprehend that question, and since I feel a pang of pain right through my chest, causing me to flinch, I don't attempt to.

Amy cocks her head to one side, looks at me with a slight squint; her long-sightedness coming into play. "You look like you've been dragged through a hedge backwards."

Again, I say nothing.

Then I think of something meaningful.

And I get it out.

"Where's AA?" I say.

" 'AA?' " she replies, complete with whimsical voice, as if she's never *heard* of him before, as if I didn't leave him to *babysit* her. "Oh, he's here too," she says.

When I rest my hands on the concrete floor, I feel a flash of pain through my palms, where I landed when I threw myself out of the moving car. I suck my teeth, but that only brings out a flaming-hot sensation in my ribs.

I glare up at Amy. "Is he . . . *part* of this?" I manage to get out.

Amy purses her lips. She flashes a smile at me, and then, hands still stuffed in the pockets of her overcoat, turns her back, as if observing some 'darling' detail of my windowless, concrete prison cell. "No," she replies, "not really."

I can't say that I think much of that qualifier . . .

"That is," Amy continues, "not *knowingly* . . . but he did act like a fool, taking the façade for reality."

I feel my stomach give a lurch.

My vision swills before me.

Almost as if the room's tilting.

I wonder if somebody gave me a whack over the head while I was passed out.

I hope not.

"Is he . . ." I take a sharp breath, feel the pain, push it down, *deep* into my stomach ". . . *like me?*"

"Is he 'like' you?" she repeats, turning back around.

She keeps her hands stuffed in her pockets.

In a way that's making me *deeply* uneasy.

"Yes," Amy finally gets out, "unfortunately, he's *just* like you, which is to say that he's loyal to Brian." She sniffs a laugh. "Pitiful *really*—I mean you're just like any other freelancer to him . . . they come and go"—here she removes her hand from the pocket of her overcoat, to show me the gun: Mrs Pietersen's gun —"*live* and *die*," she finishes, pointing the gun at my forehead.

———

Outside, in the corridor, I can hear more voices.

For some reason—for some *stupid* reason—I expect Brian to show his face, to turn up in this . . . wherever I am.

As I sit there, slumped against the wall, with Mrs Pietersen's gun pointed at my head, I catch a whiff of salt on the stilted, recycled air. I wonder if I'm close to a kitchen. If this is some sort of a top-secret hide-out.

Instead, though, the person who appears in the doorway is a bald man.

He is large, with a puffed-out chest.

No neck.

About in his mid-fifties.

He wears a knitted sweatshirt over a pair of saggy, blue jeans; that style of jean which late middle-aged men seem to be so keen on.

But my eyes slip downwards—to the *much* more important sight at his belt.

His handgun.

Slipped into its holster.

"What you doin', love?" the man says.

That same Glaswegian accent from before.

I look to Amy, and then to the man standing in the doorway.

Only when I spot those sapphire-blue eyes does something click at the back of my brain.

That they're father and daughter.

That the man standing here—the *bald* man—is none other than Charles 'Charlie' Branwick.

And, all at the same time, I know that's impossible.

Because Brian Mathewson is Amy Douglas's father.

The notebook said so.

"Put the gun down, huh?" Branwick says, stepping into the room, and turning his back on Amy with far more confidence than I might have in a similar situation.

Turning my back on *anyone* with a gun.

Branwick runs his hand over his bald head and then steps over to me. He offers me his hand and it takes a few seconds before I realise that he's trying to help me up. When I hesitate, he snaps his fingers at me, then says, "Come on, love, ain't got all day, have I?"

I glance to Amy, who has now put the gun away . . . back into that right pocket of her overcoat I suppose . . . and I reach out for Branwick's hand.

His grip is firm but gentle, which doesn't mean that it *doesn't* hurt like absolute hell, that I don't feel the pain sweeping through me from head to toe.

But I do my best to hide it.

Back up on my feet, Branwick looks me over. He gives me a light smile. "Not feeling too sharp, huh? Well, that can't be helped, not with you runnin' all over the shop, aye?"

"No," I say, still a little taken aback by this guerrilla act of chivalry, "I suppose not."

Branwick gives a hardy nod, then he turns to Amy. His expression stiffens a touch, and he says, "All right, you go get yourself some grub, or somethin' . . . *cool down*, you hear me?"

Amy's eyes sweep over mine for a fraction of a second, and then she slips out of the room. There's none of the megalomania that dominated her gaze a matter of seconds ago. The appearance of her 'father' seems to have sent her all wide-eyed and daughter-like.

Branwick turns back to me, nods down to my mobile phone, on the floor. "You get any signal on that here?"

Feeling numb, my body still rocking with the pain in my chest, I shake my head.

"Nah," Branwick replies, "not much of a spot here." He scratches his scalp a couple of times, and I have the pleasure of seeing a couple of flakes of skin slip underneath his fingernails. With the other hand than the one he did the scratching—*thank-*

fully—he reaches a handshake out to me. "You can call me Charlie," he says.

I look at the calloused hand—*'honest hands,' just like Mark's*—and I take hold.

Give his hand a shake.

"Now, Anna," 'Charlie' says, "here's the deal." He glances back at the open doorway, as if expecting somebody to be standing there, peeping in on us. Then he looks back at me. "One of you—you or Adam—you're gonna have to die, right?"

The way he says it sends a shudder down to the pit of my gut.

"What?" I just about get out.

Charlie holds up his hand for me to hear him out, as if this is just a mild matter of technicality rather than a question of life or death. "We need to send a message," Charlie says, "a message to Brian."

I stare back into those sapphire-blue eyes of his, so much like his 'daughter's' it's uncanny.

"So"—Charlie gives a shrug—"one of you's gotta die."

Again, I feel the twinge of pain in my chest, and, more than anything, I want to get out of here, out of this windowless prison cell, back into the wide, open-aired world.

The scent of salt—of fish?—becomes almost unbearable in the stale air.

I want to pull the neck of my jumper up over my mouth and nose, but know that I can do neither. Not until I have sorted out just what's going on here.

"Why?" I say. "Why do you want to send a message?"

Once more, Charlie shrugs. "Gig's up, ain't it? Oh, aye, Brian's had a real sweet time of it, laying down these laws of his, pressing his fingertips all over the place, using me to clean up his messes." Charlie gives his bald scalp another firm scratch—this time without the payoff of flakes of skin. "That's over now"—he points at the ceiling—"message from up high, gotta put a stop to it."

Another twitch through my chest.

I suck hard at my teeth, in silent agony.

"So," Charlie continues, "way it's gonna work is that one of you's gonna die, and the other one's gonna work for me"—he jabs his chest with his thumb—"on the inside track, bring me all the gossip on what goes on within the walls of Mathewson Media." He cocks his head to one side, any trace of a smile on his lips now gone for good. "That sound fair, or what?"

I stare back at him. "The notebook," I say, "you haven't seen the notebook."

Here Charlie does break into a wry grin. "Brian bought that, aye?" He shakes his head. "That little snake in the grass—never thought that someone'd try to pull the wool over *his* eyes for once?"

"It's a fake?" I say.

"Oh, aye!" Charlie says, giving a slight chuckle.

I get that sinking sensation in my gut once again.

I think back to Amy staying at my house—to how I looked after her, how I *cared* about her . . . but now I know the truth.

Charlie takes a long breath and then blows it out again. "I'm gonna bring in your pal, Adam, in a couple of minutes, all right? And between the two's a you, you're gonna work out which one gets the bullet and which one gets to play the part, okay?"

He turns to head out of the room.

Although I know there should be just about a million other things on my mind—that, *for one*, I should be silently plotting how the hell I'm going to get out of this place—I can't help but feel the question float to the top of my mind.

"Amy," I say, "why didn't you use her? Why didn't you think to use her to spy on Brian?"

"Oh, I did," Charlie replies, "all of it was going along quite smoothly, thank you very much, until Brian sussed what was going on—caught a whiff of something. That was the master-stroke with that beautiful forgery: the notebook." He taps his nose. "A wily little insurance plan you might like to call it. Set a doubt in his mind." He reaches out and gives me a playful punch on the upper arm . . . that sends a searing-hot pang right to the middle of my chest. "You're a bright girl, Anna, you'll be just the snitch we're lookin' for if that's the way you and Adam decide it."

Chapter Thirty-Six

WHEN 'CHARLIE' LEAVES THE ROOM, bringing the door shut behind him, I feel as if my blood itself is on fire. It pumps through my body—seemingly at double speed. The surface of my skin goes cold, like the skin of a freshly banked fish. The stench of salt in the air gets thicker still and I pray that they're not going to bring me through any sort of food.

I'd only bring it right back up.

And I don't want to give them the pleasure of seeing that.

That they've managed to get the better of me.

I might be down, but I'm not out.

Yet.

True to his word, Adam—*AA*—is prodded in through the doorway, and into my room.

He's dressed in a black, V-necked t-shirt, and a pair of black jeans.

Although this is hardly the time or place, I can't help

wondering if, on the day of his kidnap, AA coordinated right down to his underwear.

I can tell from how his hair sticks up in tufts that he hasn't had the chance for a good wash in several days.

The door slams shut behind him, but I'm sure that we're being monitored somehow.

AA looks me up and down, then says, "You look like shit."

Despite myself, I break out in a smile.

I stop myself short of laughing because it just hurts too damn much.

"When'd they bring you in then?" I say, each word setting me in fresh agony.

AA looks about the room. "I think a little after I sent that text to you." He looks back to me, fixes his eyes onto mine. "You know, the one about me taking Amy somewhere *you* wouldn't be able to hurt her?"

"Well," I say, "it worked."

"Yeah, a little too well if anything."

"So," I say, with a slight sigh, "which one of us is going to bite the bullet?"

"Anna!" AA replies. "*Please.*"

"Come on," I say, "we've got to talk practicalities . . . that's why they've put us here, in this room together."

It's then that AA surprises me, he takes a step towards me, wraps his arms about me.

I have no time to tell him about my ribs as he holds me tight to his rigid, well-toned body. To begin with, I think this is a sort of fatalistic gesture, when he leans in, to whisper in my ear, "Right when they turned on me—when they went to your house, couldn't get hold of you—Brian sent me a message." He pauses for a second, squeezes me tighter, and sets me in fresh agony. "He wanted me to *kill* Amy."

It's then that AA breaks off the impromptu hug, takes a step back, squares his shoulders, and sighs outwardly.

I realise that I must've been standing for a good few moments with my mouth wide open, looking like some illustrated dictionary's definition of 'shocked,' before I catch myself.

I turn my gaze downwards, to the cement at my feet.

My heart thumps along.

Shallow beats of pain pass through my chest.

But I can't help thinking to myself:

Brian knows.

He knows Amy's not his daughter.

Why else would he have called for a hit on her?

That does give me fresh hope, and I—*no joke*—feel it tingling all the way to the very tips of my toes. And then I think back to the message which Brian sent me, back at the Winged Women's Institute. The one which told me to 'take care' . . . I look down at my mobile now, lying there, dead on battery: useless. Why couldn't he have told me?

Why did he leave me out of the loop on this?

When I meet AA's eyes, he moves into me once more.

Coming back for another hug.

He presses his lips—slightly moist, his breath stilted, a little cheesy—against my ear. "Ditched my phone, right before they got to me. Never had a chance to read the message. Never found out that *Brian* knew. They think they've got him beaten. But they're wrong."

I have a go of my own, pressing my lips up against *his* earlobe. "Do you think Brian's coming—do you think he's got a plan?"

"Dunno," AA replies, his lips leaving my ear, "but I do."

AA looks away from me now.

When I glance over my shoulder, I realise why.

Amy Douglas stands in the doorway.

Once more with Mrs Pietersen's gun in her hand.

Pointing it at us.

We both hold up our hands.

"All right," Amy says, "which one of you is going to die?"

Chapter Thirty-Seven

AMY DOUGLAS'S sapphire-blue eyes swish between me and AA, like a cat's tail, thrashing about, its state of mind hardly contained as it thinks through the killing blow.

I stare at Mrs Pietersen's gun, clutched in Amy's hand.

The dark hole at the end of it.

AA glances to me, his hands—like mine—still raised, and then he looks to Amy.

Guess it's time to see this 'plan' of his grind into action.

"You won't do it, Amy," AA says.

Amy stares AA down. She wrinkles her nose, that bunny-rabbit trick of hers all over again. She squeezes the grip of the gun tighter, and I really wish AA wouldn't say anything at all. It seems that the slightest of sounds will set her off.

"No?" Amy says, her lips curling, "And why would you think that?"

"Because you don't have it in you," AA replies, "you simply don't have the killing instinct."

"You don't have a Kill Switch," I mutter to myself, and, only when Amy glances over to me, do I realise that I spoke a little too loudly.

Creases appear in Amy's forehead. She gives a shake of her head. "It's fine," she says, "I *can* do it. When the people *deserve* to die."

I think back to that disastrous hit me and Amy shared, think back about how she got all nervous, and how she *insisted* that she be the one to go through with the act. At the time, I believed that it had to do with impressing Brian . . . now, though, I realise that it was only to show herself, that she could easily take the life of somebody *innocent*—or someone 'innocent,' as far as she knew.

"We deserve to die?" AA says, hands still in the air.

Amy scoffs, cocks her head to one side. "Of course you do— you're *bad* people." Her voice tightens. "Hired *killers*."

AA softens his voice, apparently sensing that he's in danger of sending Amy's already bad mood boiling right over. "But we're your friends, Amy." He shifts a glance in my direction. "Don't you remember how Anna took you in, how the two of you shared all those good times together?"

Amy shrugs. "It was only part of the plan—part of the plan we had to put into place so that we could get Brian where we wanted him."

AA's eyes sear in their sockets. "And you have Brian where you want him now?"

A slight smile tugs at the corners of Amy's lips. "Absolutely," she says.

AA looks to me, seemingly out of ideas.

I can already feel a sigh dawning on me, the knowledge that *I'm* going to have to be the one to do something here, when, out of nowhere, AA surges forward, off his mark, rushing for Amy, head bowed, like a stampeding bull.

There's a deafening gunshot.

Another.

Then another.

Not from Amy's gun.

From the doorway.

I watch on, stunned by the spectacle, as AA wrestles Amy down to the ground, pins her with his knees on her stomach. He presses her wrists down hard against the concrete, attempting to work the gun free from Amy's hand.

During this struggle, though, he does have the presence of mind to glance back over his shoulder, to slip me a flash of the eyebrows and say, "Anna? A little help do you think?"

I break out of my daze, step forward, that jangling pain in my chest now only an unpleasant tingling sensation. I guess that it's the adrenalin kicking in.

I don't need any more orders from AA to know what I'm supposed to be doing.

I turn my attention to Mrs Pietersen's gun clutched in Amy's hand.

I work her fingers free—*one by one*—from the grip.

I feel the steady weight of the 9mm hang down at my side.

Something feels a little off about it—something at the back of my mind nagging me.

But there's no time to think, because a voice, from out in the corridor, barks out to me.

I turn to look.

Stare at the doorway.

I see Charlie standing there, his own handgun clutched tight in his fist.

The Chief Constable . . . though he's strictly off-duty right now.

At least I *hope* he is.

"Toss it, aye?" Charlie says.

I think through my options, but realise that, out in the corridor, I can already hear the stamping of boots. The throbbing overexcitement of male voices barking to one another.

There's no way out of this.

Not now.

I glance down at AA, who lets his weight up off Amy.

Using her palms, Amy scrabbles away from him.

She stumbles back up to her feet.

Arrives back beside her father, in the doorway, half hiding behind his shoulder.

AA stays down on the ground, on his knees. I can see that there's a sticky patch of blood at his side, coming through his black t-shirt. He stares long and hard, right into Charlie's eyes, and he says, "Me—take *me!*"

Chapter Thirty-Eight

CHARLIE FLIPS A GLANCE at AA, then back at me. I wait for him to tell me to drop the gun again, but I know that's simply not an option.

No clean way out of here now.

Only bullets and blood.

I bring the gun up in my grasp, aim for his forehead.

Pull the trigger.

Nothing happens.

I pull it again.

Again, nothing.

I mutter a swearword to myself, look to Charlie, see that he's grinning.

"What's the matter, eh? Not got any bullets?"

I glance over the gun, see that the safety's very much switched off—no rookie errors for me today . . . at least not *that* rookie error.

I look back to Charlie, who nods for me to check out the gun some more.

I pull out the clip.

Just like he said:

Empty.

"All the same," Charlie says, still smiling, his goons now out there, in the corridor, at his heels, "toss the gun, aye?"

I think it through, look to AA, there on his knees, hands clasped over his scalp, offering himself up like some sort of a sacrificial lamb. I'm not sure how much more of this I can take.

Out in the hallway, I see more guns being drawn.

There's no way out.

Not for me and AA—not *now*.

I toss the gun, as Charlie asks, and it lands with a *clatter* down at my feet.

I'll have to break the news of how I managed to lose Mrs Pietersen's gun to her later.

If I'm still alive, that is.

"Dad?" Amy says, standing at Charlie's side.

"What?" Charlie replies, not taking his eyes off me or AA . . . not for a second.

"Why didn't you tell me the gun was empty?" Amy says. "Didn't you *trust* me?"

Charlie rolls his eyes. "Don't be silly," he says, "I just didn't want you to have blood on your hands."

"But I already do . . . I've done it already."

I feel my chest tighten—another one of those searing-hot prickling sensations.

Jabbing into my skin.

Charlie gives a shake of his head. "No," he says, "I've got to be the one to do it—you have no idea how much trouble these two have given me over the years, how long I've waited for this moment, to have the two of them to myself."

It's then, my hands reaching for the air, in surrender, though I have no idea why, that I observe Amy's hand go to the left pocket of her overcoat. She brings her fist out from within, clutching something . . . something . . . *grey* . . . ugly-shaped . . .

Before I have a chance to say anything, to give any sort of a warning, Amy tears off the tab, and lobs the object into the room.

Chapter Thirty-Nine

INSTANTLY, smoke pours out from within, smothering us all.

Taking away our vision.

That bitter, sulphuric taste.

It catches at the back of my mouth.

There're a couple of gunshots.

One I feel whizz right by my ear.

The sound of stamping feet.

Shouts.

Charlie's voice.

On instinct, I get down on my knees, force myself beneath the level of the smoke, where the smoke hasn't yet reached.

Another few gunshots.

Someone cries out in pain.

I reach out into the smog, grab hold of AA's t-shirt, drag him before me.

My chest throbs again.

I wince long and hard, but force myself onwards.

In my mind's eye, I already have the room all scoped out.

The doorway ahead of us.

AA isn't much more good than a dead weight.

We make it through the stumbling feet, the swearwords ripping through the air.

When I get to the doorway, manage to dodge several men who rush on inside—into the room, looking to get hold of either me or AA—I feel a light touch against my cheek.

I flinch.

I look through the thickening smoke, can just about make out the fingers through my streaming eyes. When I breathe in, I feel the burning right down to the pit of my stomach.

"This way," the voice says.

Amy's voice.

She grabs hold of my hand, interlocking her fingers with my own, guiding me along, away from the madness within the room.

In turn, like a group of blinded soldiers on a battlefield, I guide AA along behind me, keep him from bumping into the wall.

We continue along the corridor, away from the smog.

When we turn the corner, I take in the grim, grey concrete walls which spring up on either side. Over our shoulders, I can still hear the cries. Those goons of Charlie's all attempting to capture us, with no idea that we've already fled.

I glance back at AA, see that he's holding his side, where he was shot. His eyes are slightly wild, and they cling to mine, like a wounded animal desperately seeking help and yet unable to obtain it.

Too *proud* to obtain it.

"Come on," Amy says, leading us along the corridor, and

then to a steel door with a ventilation hatch stamped down near its base. She fumbles about in the pocket of her overcoat, brings up a set of keys, slips one of the keys into the lock.

The hinges creak out as she opens the door, and I turn to AA, see that he's grimacing in pain still. I grab hold of him, realising that I'm going to have to be the Big Girl here, and nearly throw him into the cubby hole.

A ladder leads upwards.

Into the gloom above.

Right as Amy stands at the door, ready to slam it shut, she looks me in the eye, and says, "That'll lead you up—back to the surface. Get as far along the shore as you can manage. Then get into contact with Brian . . . he'll know what to do."

The prospect of the 'shore' continues to jangle about my brain, when I turn on Amy, a thousand questions on my lips, but only one surfacing as a fully developed string of words. "What about you?" I say, my brow furrowed.

But, before she can reply, she slams the door shut on us.

Leaving me and AA to the darkness.

And the ladder.

———

Just as promised, after a climb of about a minute or so—with AA clambering up in front of me—we come up to a hatch. Daylight shines down through the opening: sunset, dawn; I couldn't care less. As I cling to the rungs of the ladder, I feel as if somebody is constantly stabbing me in the chest.

AA glances back down at me, makes some moaning noises about 'not having the strength' to bust it open. But a good, old-fashioned, steely glare is all it takes to change his mind.

Grimacing, he shoulder barges the hatch open.

With another series of grunts, he lugs himself through the gap, and back up to ground level. I follow him out, surely feeling a similar amount of pain but not making such a great deal about it.

What *is it* about men and pain?

They seem to have to suffer through *everything* . . .

Me and AA stumble our way out, and, sure enough, I spy the shore, the mouth of a river up ahead. "The Thames," AA manages to get out, in gasping tones.

Sure enough, I note the sewage-brown water spilling out from the mouth of the river, into the grey-blue sea. I look over, across at the horizon, seeing the sun rising up, its rays all sparkling against the lackadaisical waves.

On the air, I can smell the salt, and that ugly fishy stench:

The one I smelled down there, in that . . . *bunker?*

I glance along the pebble beach just out ahead, and can't help but hear a sort of throbbing in my ears. At first I think it's my heart, threatening to break out through my ribs while they're still weak—still in *constant* pain—but when I see AA turn his head to look off, in the direction of the sound, I realise that it's not only happening within the realm of my own skull.

For a change.

I hear the blades thrashing through the sky.

Beating against the air.

Defying gravity and—*I'm sure*—a whole host of other forces that I couldn't name.

The helicopter sweeps into view, over the sea, its blades sending the surface of the water scurrying in a series of ripples.

For several seconds, I feel somewhat confused, unsure how

this has happened, how *anybody* beyond Charlie Branwick and his goons knew where I was.

And then I recall my mobile phone.

I think back to what Amy said, about being able to find anybody you want if you try hard enough.

I look back to AA, then say, "Looks like Brian came for us after all."

AA gives me a slight wince, still gripping his side, where Charlie shot him.

Feeling the tight pain in my own chest, I roll my eyes at him. "Cheer up," I say, "at least it wasn't me who shot you this time, huh?"

Chapter Forty

TWO WEEKS LATER, I sit at my kitchen table, brewing a teapot.

The gentle, sweet odour sweeps through the air; blowing all my cares away with it.

It's a bit of a cold snap, and nothing beats being inside my nicely heated house with the knowledge that the only things which linger in my immediate future are warm drinks and sugary snacks.

I feel Lizzie come up to my leg; rub herself a touch seductively against me.

Realising that she's not looking for food—*for once*—I take hold of her chubby frame, and plump her down in my lap. I glance to my mobile, checking for any message from Mark.

Last night, we had a long—*long*—conversation; about Life, Death, and Everything. He filled me in about how his chat with Nathan went; the one where he had to tell Nathan that, actually, contrary to what Nathan previously thought, Mark isn't his biological father.

Nathan took it fine, which is to say that he took it as well as a child might be expected to take news like that. A little bit of sulking, some tantrums, threats to run away . . . that sort of thing. I can't help thinking that Mark's had his hands just as full as mine have been in the past couple of weeks, what with the medical check-ups; the toing-and-froing from the hospital; along with keeping my child-visitation duties up to bare minimum:

Doing my best to stay out of either my ex-husband—Arnold —and his partner—Kate's—reach as far as possible.

But I did manage to take Ben and Josie to the zoo one day.

They seemed to enjoy it, in a slightly too-grown-up-for-this sort of way.

Things seem to be going well with Mark, though.

Very Well Indeed.

I can see him sticking around for a while . . . just as long as none of those skeletons he was so fond of chatting about don't come wandering out of the closet.

I reach up to my chest, feeling for the padding I have there— the *bandages*.

Brian's doctor informed me that I've cracked three ribs, and he was most stern about how I'd obviously exacerbated my injuries before seeking out professional medical advice. Although I did catch the impression that Brian's doctor was not unused to being sent along strange specimens such as myself; and AA; it didn't seem to affect his judgement any.

Perhaps he's of the belief that Brian's PAs routinely get themselves involved in shoot-outs and the like.

Maybe he just tells himself lies.

To make himself feel better.

Although the doctor prescribed me a whole host of pills to take, with a quick run through the internet, I identified which were the painkillers and quickly weeded those out of the mix. Because I know someone like me needs to stay sharp at all times.

Be ready and prepared to kill.

While AA was lying flat on his hospital bed, getting those bullets tugged out of him, he had plenty of time to tell me how Amy turned and told him that I'd tried to endanger her life—that I'd had a chance to save her from getting mauled by the dog, and done nothing.

AA—like an *idiot*—had believed Amy.

Or at least her panic.

Straight or gay, men do seem to be a soft touch around a crying woman . . .

He also filled me in on the diary. That while Brian *had* given Amy's mother the diary one Christmas, she had never got around to using it. When this situation had come up, Amy had ingeniously decided to make mock entries, rendering her mother's handwriting the best she could.

Making up lies which would unnerve Brian.

I hear a knock at my door—someone *politely* preferring not to use the bell.

I lift Lizzie up off my lap, she gives me that *miaow* of protest, and I go to answer.

Standing there, as arranged, is Mrs Pietersen.

It's somewhat strange to see her not wearing a pinny apron for once.

Today she has on a mustard-coloured dress with flower prints sketched all over.

A neat and, quite pretty, textile belt around the waist.

She has a much better figure than I noticed earlier on.

In her hands, she carries a delicious-looking carrot cake with vanilla icing.

A carrot painstakingly iced onto the top.

Already I feel my stomach give a slight jiggle of anticipation.

She smiles at me, the wrinkles about her eyes becoming thinner and deeper. "Thought you might have a sweet tooth."

"You thought right," I say, stepping to one side, to allow Mrs Pietersen in over the threshold.

I lead her through to the kitchen and I notice Lizzie leap off my chair, where she'd been taking advantage of the warmed-up wooden seat.

Lizzie trots up neatly to Mrs Pietersen, rubs herself against Mrs Pietersen's bare calf.

I take the carrot cake off Mrs Pietersen so that she might make a fuss of Lizzie.

While Mrs Pietersen takes her seat at the kitchen table, Lizzie strutting about her lap, purring away, I tend to the tea, pouring out a pair of even cups. I pour in a little splash of milk; and a dash of sugar, then give each of the mugs a good stirring.

I thought that telling Mrs Pietersen the truth might be difficult, but, in the end, it was much easier than I imagined. Of course, I didn't tell her the *real* truth, but just enough so that, next time she sees AA skulking about the place, she won't pick up the phone and call the police . . . though I do hope she'll think twice about handing him over my house keys.

I let her know that the men who got into my house were somewhat overeager bailiffs, that they were working for the owner of my house—Mrs Pietersen, thankfully, doesn't know that *I* am the owner of my own house.

I tell her about how I got behind on payments, a silly thing really: cash-flow issues; and I had been looking for some way out; off the property.

When she asked me what my job was, I cryptically replied 'investor' and she at least greeted the term with raised eyebrows and a latched-open mouth.

I hope that'll go some way to explaining away the night-time departures; the early-morning arrivals.

Or not.

After having apologised profusely for having abused of the misunderstanding; and, coupled with the cheque for the Winged Women's Institute I showed her, she seemed convinced I wasn't a total psychopath.

Fooled her . . .

I asked her over today so that we could have a cup of tea. It seems like Mrs Pietersen could use a little human company just as much as I could.

Somewhat ironic that we've both been using Lizzie as our common piece of company.

I hand Mrs Pietersen over her cup of tea and she takes it from me with a wide smile, and a whispered, "Thank you."

It's right then, just as I'm on the point of sinking down into the chair opposite Mrs Pietersen, and getting something done about cutting into the carrot cake, that something catches the corner of my eye.

Outside.

A sleek, purple estate car with tinted windows.

Not quite a stretch-limo.

But getting there.

I'd know that car anywhere.

Although I wish, more than anything, that I didn't.

I shine a smile on Mrs Pietersen. "Would you excuse me for a moment?"

"Of course," Mrs Pietersen says, placing her tea cup back down on the table, and sticking her hands back in Lizzie's fur, setting her off purring all over again.

———

I slip a denim jacket off the coat rack in the hall—a recent acquisition—and slip out through the front door, very much aware that Mrs Pietersen will be watching my every movement, with those gossipy eyes of hers, through the kitchen window.

But if she does, then who *cares?*

I told her that I often have face-to-face meetings with various odds and sods about town, and that—*sometimes*—they show up on my doorstep.

I really hope that this doesn't become a game; that I don't end up pushing my luck too far in seeing just how much bullshit I can get Mrs P to buy.

The door to the back seat of the car is already open, and I look into the gloom. Without so much as seeing a face within, I say, "I've got company—can this wait till later?"

"Just a word, Anna," Brian says, from out of the obscurity. "Promise it won't take a moment."

I glance about me and, sure enough, see Mrs Pietersen's face in the window of the kitchen. I wave back to her and give her a —*hopefully*—carefree smile, which, at the very least, sends her away from the glass.

I could really do *without* Ursula showing up again to take me away to the Winged Women's Institute.

I slip inside the car, land with a soft *plump* on the leather seat.

The floor's much shallower than I thought, or maybe it's just that the seat's reclined further back than I anticipated.

I look over Brian's features—see that he's smiling from ear to ear.

I'm so *glad* that he has *something* to be happy about.

"What is it?" I say.

"Shut the door, please, Anna," he says.

I think long and hard about stepping out of the car, just leaving Brian there, with his own messes, but, in the end, I do close the door behind me.

What's that expression?

In for a penny, in for a pound.

I glance up, see that the driver's kept apart from us by one of those interior, tinted, apartheid windows. All I can make out is the back of the driver's thick neck. His close-cropped hair. I can't even get a good look at his body.

Brian really *is* a meanie sometimes . . .

I look to Brian's hands and see, sure enough, that he clutches his signature tumbler of whisky. When my eyes adjust a little more to the gloom, I realise that his cheeks are slightly rosy.

Somebody's been celebrating.

"I expect you've been waiting for this, Anna."

"Waiting for what?"

"The debrief—to see that all your work came good?"

"What work?" I say. "Because, forgive me for saying, but I can't quite remember being on the clock for a sizeable portion of it."

Brian smirks a touch. "Oh, Anna, you said it yourself—it's not about the money." He pauses, draws out the silence for a tense few seconds. "A kind of *therapy*—an *outlet.*"

"A way to let off my Kill Switch."

"Right," Brian says, grinning all over, and sending a waft of whisky over in my direction. He slides his knees up a little bit, and I see that he's wearing a silky, black suit, with a white shirt. He looks a touch formal for a Saturday, but, then again, Brian Mathewson isn't really the sort who does anything by halves.

"Is there anything you'd like to ask?" Brian says. "Any loose ends you'd like me to"—he pauses for a moment, apparently to stifle a burp with the back of his hand—"*tie up?*"

"Charlie Branwick," I say, "what happens to him?"

"Charlie?" Brian says, with a Big, Fat Smile. "Yes, a touch concerning for him, professionally speaking, I'm afraid."

"And why's that?"

"Lost his job, poor soul," Brian says, sounding genuinely dejected for all of a millisecond. He brightens again, takes another swig of his whisky, draining the glass.

"What'll happen?" I say. "Didn't he have some . . . you know, *information?*"

Brian gives me a sly glance, the wrinkles about his eyes creasing up. "You sound just a little involved for a hired killer, don't you think?"

I shrug "Seems like I always get wrapped up in stuff, doesn't it?"

Brian pouts then gives a nod. "I suppose you would be right in saying that." He stares into the base of his now-empty whisky glass, in the same way, I imagine, a sinful priest regrets and repents. "The information," he continues, "I had to give them something—something to go on."

I strain my mind, think back to when I saw Amy the first time . . . in her new guise. "She was doing something with the computer," I say, "something with a USB stick."

Brian gives a doleful nod. "Yes, I'm afraid she was—as I'd

hoped she might do." He breathes out a sigh. "You see, I'd suspected for quite a while, the first time that Charlie came to me, in fact, with the revelation that his daughter wanted to get in on the assassins' gig, that it might be an attempt at espionage. I know all the sacrifices Charlie has made for me—all the strings he's pulled in the name of our friendship. All those times we've shared in the past."

I feel a twinge through my chest.

I try not to show any sign of pain, but, in the end, it's impossible not to.

Brian gives me a smile. "Those ribs healing up okay?"

Unable to catch my breath for several moments, I settle on only giving him a nod.

"Hmm," Brian says, really to himself, then continues, "Charlie would always get his cut, of course, but I suppose there comes a time in a man's life when other virtues take precedent—when the number in the bank account just doesn't seem to matter as much anymore . . . not as much as the respect of one's colleagues"—Brian meets me with a laser stare—"the respect of one's *enemies.*"

"You gave Amy . . . I mean, in the office, when you had me and Amy meet, you wanted it so that she would go delving about that computer?"

Brian smiles at me. "You could put it that way—I needed to give Charlie something so that he thought he was onto a winner, having his daughter spy on my operation."

"What was on the USB stick—what did she take?"

Brian gives a shrug. "Some things of minor importance, pieces of a puzzle that won't make a whole lot of sense without the whole to work from. That was why Charlie needed one of you."

I can't say that Brian's words totally assure me . . . but I guess it's all that I'm going to get for the time being. I feel my throat drying up, already knowing that it's *well* beyond my business to ask the next question.

But I do so anyway.

"The diary?" I say. "Were you taken in by it?"

Brian breathes out steadily. He begins to shake his head, and then stops. His whole body seems to go stiff. He slips me a side-long glance. "No," Brian says, and then, apparently correcting himself, "Not after I'd done some due diligence."

I wonder what he might precisely mean by this, and then I assume—*most likely*—he got hold of some of Amy Douglas's DNA . . . not a tricky task for someone of Brian's resources; though it certainly *does* strike me as being somewhat creepy.

"I couldn't contact you directly," Brian says, "not while you were on the run—it would've been too risky. By the time I got in touch with Adam about terminating Amy, it was too late for him. Speaking of which"—Brian thrusts a finger up in the air, he digs about in a black, canvas bag which sits at his feet, produces a bundle which he holds out to me—"Merry Christmas," he utters.

I take the items from him. "Few months to go yet," I say, and then examining the contents, drawing back the cloth, I see both Mrs Pietersen's gun there; along with old, trusty *Punisher*, my .45 from that hit, way back when. I look back at Brian. "Thanks," I say.

Brian just gives me a nod. "Guess we'll be in touch, then, Anna?"

"Guess so," I say, sliding my way across the leather surface of the back seat, returning to the door, and the outside air.

Only when I stand outside the car, feel the stiff, numbing winter wind blast against my cheeks, stripping away any moisture, do I realise how badly the back of the car stank.

All that whisky; it really can't be good for a man.

I watch the car swoop around the corner, and out of sight.

When I glance back across the façade of my house, there's nobody peering out through the kitchen windows. No sign of Mrs Pietersen spying on my impromptu meeting, but, then again, perhaps she knew to slip away as I was alighting.

Back inside, I see that Mrs Pietersen hasn't been shy in serving herself a couple of thick slices of carrot cake. She turns to me, her cheeks glowing—not like Brian's, with alcohol, but with warmth, with *companionship*.

I take the seat opposite her, not thinking of the bundles I hold.

And which I lay down on the table between us.

"What've you got there?" Mrs Pietersen says.

I feel a tingle through my chest, but don't panic.

There's no need to panic now.

I give a shake of my head. "An early Christmas present," I reply.

"I'll say," Mrs Pietersen responds, "there's a good few weeks to go still."

Then something in my mind snaps, and I recall.

I fish through the bundle of rags, my fingers working over the guns. "Actually," I say, revealing the contents of the rags to her, "there's something for you too."

Mrs Pietersen, the smile on her lips dialling down a couple of notches, looks to her gun, to the 9mm service pistol she handed me, for my own protection.

Since she doesn't make a move for it, I lift it up and pass it to her.

She takes it from me, her hands shaking.

Then, after she's analysed the gun she holds in her own hands, she turns her attention to the last remaining one: to *Punisher*. This time, the old, familiar smile returns to her lips. "Seems like you're nicely catered for there."

I meet her eye, smile back. "Guess you could say that."

Soon after, the two of us fall about giggling, unable to contain ourselves.

And we spend a good afternoon, eating cake, chatting about everything and anything; and passing Lizzie between the two of us.

And not one mention of killing.

Let alone my Kill Switch.

THE END

Author's Note

Thank you for taking the time to read one of my books. If you would like to hear about my latest releases you can sign up for my newsletter here: www.aviain.com

Thanks for reading!

AV Iain

Kill Switch
The Third Anna Harris Novel